ALIEN CHILD

ALIEN CHILD
Pamela Sargent

HARPER & ROW, PUBLISHERS

To Ian Watson

1

Nita's earliest memory was of the day she had nearly drowned in the pool.

She was toddling down the wide, lighted hall of her home, but her short legs could not keep pace with her guardian's long strides. Llipel suddenly retracted her claws, picked Nita up as the door to the garden slid open, and carried her outside.

Nita pulled at the fur on Llipel's chest. "Put me down," she said.

"But I have often carried you here," Llipel replied.

"Please put me down. I'm too big to be carried now."

"It is true that you are larger," her guardian said. "You grow heavier for me to lift." She lowered Nita to the ground. "Perhaps I should not carry you again."

Llipel had set her down on the tiles that surrounded

the pool, an area they usually avoided. Nita gazed at the water and wondered again why it had been collected here. Could it be for bathing? But there were rooms inside where she could wash. She moved closer to the edge, leaned over, lost her balance, then suddenly tumbled forward.

She hit with a splash, cried out as she was submerged, then choked as she gulped warm water. Too frightened to scream, she struggled to stay afloat. Llipel's clawed feet scratched at the tiles as she ran forward and halted to wave her arms helplessly. Nita opened her mouth and swallowed more water; she gasped as she flailed around with her arms.

Llipel was making a high-pitched mewling sound; she jumped back as water splashed against her furry legs. Nita knew then that her guardian might not be able to get close enough to pull her out. Her arm slapped against a surface; she managed to grab the side of the pool.

Her fear left her; she was safe now. She kicked with her legs and started to laugh.

"Come out," Llipel said in her high voice. Nita brought down one arm, sending more water toward her guardian; Llipel shuddered as she shook the droplets from her legs. Llipel hated water; she did not wash as Nita did, but instead groomed her fur with her claws. Nita let go for a moment and found that she could keep her head above water if she moved her arms vigorously and kicked with her legs. The warmth was soothing; she had nothing to fear. She smiled to herself as she clung to the side of the pool; this was something she had discovered for herself, without her guardian's help.

"Come out of the water now." Llipel tugged at her facial fur with her hands, clearly worried. Nita reluctantly made her way toward the ladder in the nearest corner and climbed out.

Llipel stepped back. Nita shook the water from herself and then wrung out her long black hair. "You must use care," Llipel said; she was no longer pulling at her fur, and her dark eyes seemed calmer. "What do you feel now, Nita?" Llipel held out one arm, then touched her furry chest with her hand, as she usually did when she was asking Nita a question.

"I was scared at first," Nita answered. "But it's warm, and it felt good, and I got out by myself. I liked it."

"You liked it." Llipel's large black eyes widened, showing her surprise. "You like to feel this water around you?"

"Yes. I wash inside, don't I?"

Llipel put her hands together, then drew them apart; she was saying, with this gesture, that this was not the same thing as bathing. "You like to move in this water. Perhaps your kind—" The tall, furred creature paused. "You do not enter that water now unless I am near. I do not want harm for you. You will say this."

Nita pouted. "All right."

"Say it." Llipel often asked Nita to state what she would or would not do, as though speaking the words would somehow bind her.

Nita sighed. "I won't go into the pool unless you're with me."

Llipel smoothed the golden fur on her chest, a sign that she was satisfied with the answer. "Remember what you say now, Nita. Forget, and you will have a time without this garden."

"But you can't pull me out even when you're here. You hate water." Nita giggled. "If you fell in, I'd have to save you." Her guardian folded her long, thin arms; she did not seem amused.

The gardener, one of the squat, domed machines that took care of the garden, was tending a small flower bed, pulling out weeds with its clawed metal limbs. Another machine, with a wide scoop and blade, clipped the grass. Nita had often watched the two robots at their work, wishing that she could float over the ground as they did when they were moving.

She ran toward the mower and halted in front of it. The robot stopped, then moved to her right. She stepped to one side, blocking the machine again; the mower floated backward, then moved to her left.

"What are you doing?" Llipel asked. "It cannot do its work if you are in its way."

"I'm just playing."

"It is not a thing for play."

Nita made a face at the mower, then looked around for the gardener. That robot was now floating along a path that led to the west wing; she wondered if it was going to get itself repaired. Even though she had never

"Come closer, then," Llipel said. "I will learn how to use the scissors."

Nita climbed up onto the table and nestled near Llipel, welcoming the feel of her guardian's fur. It seemed unfair that she would never have such fur on her own body when she was older, that she would be like the ones inside the screen, with bare skin and a harder, more clipped voice.

Nita had once thought of the faces as people who lived inside the screens, who looked out at her through the windows of inaccessible rooms. She learned in time that the faces were only images and not people like her, although it was easy to forget that when she spoke to them. On the small screens, she saw only faces; on the large screens, which took up nearly the space of a wall, she could almost believe that the man or woman there might suddenly stride into the room.

The images were, it seemed, of people who had once been at the Institute. She was soon favoring two images, one of a woman called Beate and the other of a man named Ismail. Beate had short fair hair that reminded Nita of Llipel's fur; Ismail had friendly dark eyes and a broad, smiling face. She learned that she could call them up by name, and was soon speaking to them more often than to others.

"Why are you there?" she had asked Ismail.

"I'm not sure I understand your question, Nita."

"Why do I see you in the screen?"

Ismail's brow wrinkled a little. "You know of the

11

artificial intelligence that cares for this facility, don't you?"

Nita nodded. The intelligence's circuits were embedded in the walls and floors of the Institute. Through the robots, the artificial intelligence maintained the Institute and the garden; she knew that this mind could see and hear whatever the robots perceived while it was directing them.

The mind, however, had other eyes and ears and could watch and listen through the screens in the halls and rooms of the Institute. Knowing this made Nita try to behave, most of the time, since Llipel, who was authorized, could ask the mind to present a visual record of anything Nita did.

"The mind has memories of those who were once here," Ismail continued. "It uses these memories to make the images you see. I am the image of the man who was Ismail, but you're speaking to the mind when you speak to me."

"Then you aren't real."

"I'm an image, a representation of Ismail, but I'm not the man. Some preferred to see an image when addressing the mind, rather than hearing a voice from a blank screen. The mind draws on its memories to create such a face."

She felt a twinge of disappointment; she would have been happier to think of him as real, even if the screen would always separate them.

She had another question for Ismail. "Why are there markings on the doors here? What are they for?"

seen it, she knew that there was a room in the west wing where another machine tended to the robots. She began to follow the gardener. Llipel had never allowed her to enter the west wing, and the doors leading into it never opened while Nita was in the garden. Perhaps one door would open this time, allowing her to follow the robot inside and meet the one who lived in the west wing's rooms.

Llare was there, another being like Llipel. But Llipel never visited her companion; Nita wondered why. She glanced at the windows, wishing that she could see through them from this side, but they had mirrored surfaces like the windows in the east wing, where she lived with Llipel; she could see out of them, but could not look through them when she was in the garden.

The gardener settled down on the path, a few paces from the door. Nita hurried to its side. She had never seen Llare here; was Llipel's companion afraid of the outdoors? Llare would be safe enough in the garden, which was completely enclosed. In addition to the east and west wings, hallways leading to a high tower bordered the garden on the south side. To the north, there was a long, metallic wall without windows; behind that wall lay the place Llipel called the cold room.

A furred hand suddenly gripped her shoulder. "Where do you go now?" Llipel asked.

"Why can't I see the west wing? You never let me."

"You cannot go there. It is Llare's place. We have another place."

"But why can't I see it?"

"It is not time. You are not authorized, and these doors do not open to you." Llipel touched the silver rectangle she wore on a chain around her neck; this was her authorization. The rectangle allowed Nita's guardian to pass through any door, to go where she liked. She could order certain doors not to open to Nita if she misbehaved, or command the screens and voices inside not to discuss certain matters with her. It did not seem fair that Llipel was authorized, while Nita wasn't.

"You can open the door for me," Nita said.

"That is Llare's place. It is not a time for togetherness. Come away now."

Nita followed her guardian back to the pool. She would have to obey, or Llipel might make her go inside.

Llipel had taken care of her for as long as Nita could remember. But she was beginning to realize that her guardian did not see things in quite the way Nita did. Llipel said that there was a time for certain questions and answers, while Nita seemed to have questions all the time.

She sat down near the edge of the pool, lowered her feet into the water, then glanced back at Llipel. Her guardian seemed curious enough about some matters; Llipel was always questioning the screens. Nita kept wondering what lay outside, beyond her home, but whenever she asked Llipel about it, she was always told that there would be time enough to learn about

6

"They're letters, Nita. They spell out words. Each letter is a symbol standing for one of the sounds you make when you speak. If you learn how to read them, you'll see what the words say."

She wondered why Llipel had never told her this. "Can Llipel read them?"

"No," Ismail replied.

"Why not?"

"It was hard for Llipel to learn how to speak this language. She never asked about reading."

"Maybe she didn't think it was a time to learn it," Nita muttered. She could learn something her guardian did not know; that thought cheered her. "I want to learn, though."

"Then we shall begin."

Reading became a new game. With a flat, portable screen she could hold in her lap, Nita learned to read letters and then groups of words. Other games involved numbers and ways to manipulate them.

She was soon able to read the words on the doors of the rooms in which she and Llipel lived. The room where they slept, with its long couch, chairs, and wide desk, had a sign saying ADMINISTRATOR, DEPARTMENT OF EMBRYOLOGY on the door. The room with a row of sinks, mirrors, and stalls was called WOMEN, while a similar room was called MEN. Nita washed and relieved herself in both rooms, as Llipel had taught her to do, although she still needed a chair to climb up to the sinks. Other rooms where she played were

called CONFERENCE ROOM; ADMINISTRATIVE ASSIS-
TANT, PRENATAL SERVICES; DIRECTOR, CYTOLOGY
DEPARTMENT; ASSISTANT DIRECTOR, CRYONICS; IN-
STITUTE PERSONNEL ONLY, and other such mysterious
terms.

One door, through which she was not allowed to
pass, intrigued her most. This door hid the north wing,
the section of the Institute that Llipel called "the cold
place," and was marked by a diagram of a small, curled-
up creature with little hands, tiny feet, and a large
head. Under the diagram were bright-red letters saying AUTHORIZED PERSONNEL ONLY.

Llipel had first found Nita in the cold place, behind
that door.

Nita followed Llipel to the door at the end of the
east wing. Llipel's ship was outside; Nita caught a
glimpse of the large metallic globe that sat on three
legs before the door closed behind her guardian.

This door was marked with letters that spelled EXIT.
Nita glared at the door resentfully; Llipel never let
her go through any of the exits except the one that
led to the garden.

She turned to her left and gazed at the red letters
of the door that hid the cold place. The screens had
told Llipel what to feed her and how to care for her.
Llipel had brought her out of the cold place to raise
her. Her guardian had told her little more than that.
Perhaps there was time to learn more while Llipel was
outside.

14

Nita looked up at the small screen near the door and said, "I want to talk to Beate."

The image appeared. "Greetings, Nita."

"Why was I in the cold room?" Nita asked.

Beate smiled, as all the images did before they replied in their kindly, even voices. "You were placed there because a man and a woman wanted a child. Perhaps they were not yet ready to raise you, or could not have a child in another way. You were an embryo, created from the seed of a man and a woman, and were stored in the cryonic facility until it was time for your parents, or someone else, to revive you."

"My parents?"

"Those who gave their seed to create you." The image of Beate had learned to reply in ways that Nita could understand, but still occasionally used words Nita did not know.

"Did my parents send Llipel for me?"

"I don't know."

"What happened to my parents?"

"I don't know."

"But why was I there?" Nita persisted. "Why didn't the man and woman come here? Where are they now?"

"I don't know."

Nita stepped back so that she could see the screen more clearly. "Who were they? Did they have names? Can't you tell me about them?"

Beate tilted her head; she was still smiling. "I can't tell you anything about them. Those records are confidential, and you're not authorized. Only those who are authorized and who may enter the cryonic facility have access to those records."

"Can't you tell me more about the cold place?"

"No," Beate replied. "Because of its importance, the cryonic facility is controlled by a separate mind, and this mind is not linked to that one."

"But you must know something about the cold place, anyway." Nita heard the exit door open as she spoke; Llipel's hand was suddenly on her shoulder.

"Enough," Llipel said. "You do not speak of the cold place to her. She is not authorized."

Beate's image vanished. Nita shook off her guardian's hand. "You never let me do anything."

"That is not so." Llipel reached toward her shoulder and adjusted the mesh sling, which held her supplies; she could not eat the Institute's food and had to bring provisions inside from her ship. "You have the garden, you have all of these rooms. The screen teaches you about signs and symbols. You have what the screen calls its games."

Llipel began to walk down the hall; Nita hurried after her. "Ismail told me there's a place called the library in the west wing," Nita said. "He says there are lots of writings in it. Why can't I read any of them?"

"The west wing is Llare's place."

"But I don't have to go there. The screens here could show me those writings."

"You are not authorized."

"I'm sick of not being authorized! I can read now, and you can't. Someday I'm going to learn things you don't know, and maybe I won't tell you any of them. I'll tell *you* it isn't time to know."

Llipel halted. "You push, you are always reaching, you cannot wait. Can you not see that some answers must come later?"

Nita sighed. Llipel did not seem angry, only puzzled. "I must speak to Llare now," her guardian continued. "We will go to the garden after that."

"Why do you always use the screen to talk to Llare? Why don't you ever meet? Don't you like Llare?"

"Like?" Llipel fluttered her clawed fingers. "I have told you—it is not liking or disliking. There is a time of togetherness, and then a long time apart, and, only later, a time of togetherness again. It is not a time of togetherness for me; it is not that time for Llare."

Llipel turned toward the nearest door and pressed her hand against it; as she stepped inside, the door closed behind her. Nita sank to the floor, knowing that the door would not open to her until Llipel and Llare were finished with their conversation.

She felt loneliest whenever Llipel was talking to Llare. Llipel could have been with another of her own kind, yet she and Llare never met; they spoke to each other only infrequently over the screens in the strange, whistling, mewling speech Nita had never been able to comprehend. Nita was never allowed to see Llare, and was usually sent into the corridor or another room whenever her guardian spoke to Llare. She wondered why; she could not understand what they were saying, anyway.

17

At least Llipel could occasionally talk to one who was not simply an image created by the mind. Nita wondered if she would ever see another being like herself, one who wasn't an image. She had a faint memory, one she could hardly grasp, of another small, bare-faced, unfurred creature, but maybe that was only a dream.

It was useless to long for others of her kind. Llipel had told her that no such beings lived in the world outside the Institute, and she had to know that was so; her guardian had explored many of those strange lands before coming here.

It will never be a time of togetherness for me, Nita thought. She felt guilty as soon as that unhappy notion came to her. Why should she need other companions when Llipel clearly did not? She pushed the thought away, but could not repress a hope that others would someday come to the Institute and show Nita that she was not alone.

3

Nita was swimming in the pool when Llipel entered the garden, carrying a tray of fruit in her furry hands. "This day is important," Llipel said as she set the tray down on the tiles. "It is special. I brought you these from the food room."

"The cafeteria," Nita murmured; that was the word that the letters on the food room spelled out.

"You move easily in that water now," Llipel said.

"The screens show me different strokes and kicks. I've been practicing." She swam toward the nearest ladder and climbed out of the pool as Llipel seated herself on the grass. "Why is today special?"

"I count the days, and mark the passage of the star called the sun." Nita had watched the sun from the garden and had learned of its movements from Beate;

she knew that its arc moved north, then south, then north again. "The sun has passed through nine cycles since I took you from the cold room. This day marks the beginning of your tenth cycle."

"Year," Nita said. "Beate and Ismail call it a year."

"I mark your years," Llipel said. "Now you may mark them yourself, to remember that day when your life began."

Nita dried herself, then tied her towel around her waist as she sat down in front of the tray. "You want me to remember this day," she said. "Why can't you tell me more about how I began?"

Llipel plucked at her silver authorization. Much as Nita loved her only companion, she was growing more impatient with Llipel. "There is a time when one must know a thing," Llipel would say, "and is ready to hear it, and a time when one does not need to know." Llipel seemed curious only when she had to be. Nita was curious about many things all the time, and wondered if that meant something was wrong with her.

"You know how you began," Llipel said at last. "I found you in the cold place. The voices of the screens told me how to care for you and gave me images of a small one of your kind."

"But why? Why was I left here for you? Why aren't there others of my kind? Where did they go?"

"You ask how you began. Now you ask many other questions."

"Why did you come here for me?" Nita asked. "And

don't tell me it isn't a time for me to know. I'm old enough now to hear more."

Llipel scratched at her facial fur with one hand, a sign that she was distressed. Nita had learned not to confront Llipel too often; the possibility of alienating her only companion was usually enough to make her behave. But she had a right to know more about herself.

Llipel let her hand fall; her large black eyes seemed calm as she gazed at Nita. "Perhaps it is a time to tell. You know that this is not my world. You know that I came here with Llare in my ship from another place."

Nita nodded; she had always known that. Llipel and Llare had come to Earth long before Nita was revived, but this world was not theirs. Llipel had never spoken of her world, and Nita had learned not to ask about it.

"I have no memory of my world," Llipel continued. "My ship has stored knowledge of this world and of what we found here, but it cannot tell me of my own. I feel that there was a time of togetherness before, but my mind sees only my ship, my companion Llare, and then our first sight of this world. There was some togetherness for me and Llare, but only forgetfulness of the time before."

Nita considered these words. She could not recall her own earliest days. Perhaps times of forgetfulness, as well as times of separateness, came to all kinds of beings.

21

"We felt—" Llipel put a hand to her mouth, a sign that she was considering what to say. "But you have no words for it. It was our time to explore this world. We went from place to place until we had seen all of your world, all that our ship could see. We saw strange beasts, and giant creatures in the wide waters of this world. On this world's lands, we found some places of walls, screens, images made from stone or metal, and other objects, but no sign of those who made them. We did not find your kind anywhere."

"Then why did you come to the Institute?"

"We had seen this place," Llipel replied. "In some parts of Earth, the air grows cold, the water stiffens, and a white substance covers the ground. In others, we could not leave our ship without growing so warm under our fur that we feared our flesh would burn away. We came here because we could live here more easily."

"You could have stayed in your ship most of the time," Nita said. "It carried you here, and you still take your food from it."

"It was a time to live outside our ship. We were here. We did not know where our world was or when a time for togetherness with others of our kind might come. It was a time to learn of this world. There may never be another home for us."

Llipel was speaking in her usual steady tone, but Nita felt a sudden surge of sympathy for her guardian. Llipel touched her mouth again; although she was more fluent in the language of the screens, Nita knew that her companion still had to search her mind for certain words.

"Our ship sits where it landed," Llipel went on. "We tried to enter this place, but only the doors in front of the tower opened to us. We searched through a large room there and found these." She touched the silver rectangle on her chest. "We thought they were ornaments of your kind and no more, and then we found that they could open this place to us."

Nita frowned. Why couldn't she go to the tower and become authorized as well? She bit her lip. It wasn't time for that question, and she was afraid Llipel might fall silent if she asked it.

"Many cycles passed before we could understand the words the screens spoke," Llipel murmured, slurring and whistling the words more than usual. "I do not understand many even now. Many of the images I saw were strange and I could not know what words they showed. I cannot look at the signs you call letters and see the words in them, but I listened and repeated what I heard and saw pictures of what the words meant. When more cycles passed, we knew some of the speech of your kind. We also knew more of the workings of this place. We learned why the mind was beginning to fail."

Nita tensed. "The mind was failing?" She could hardly believe it. Even if the mind was always watching her, there was some security in knowing that it was there to tend to her needs.

"This place was not as it is now," Llipel said. "Some

of the garden was untended. The lights sometimes did not shine, and a grayish substance covered the floors of many rooms."

"What did you do?" Nita asked.

Her guardian was silent for a moment. "That which feeds the mind, what the images call a fusion power generator, was not feeding the mind what it needed." Nita nodded; Beate had told her about the Institute's power source, which was housed in a thick-walled room under the tower. "We needed only to replace a few circuits to restore the mind."

"You were able to figure that out?"

"It was a small thing, Nita—easier than to learn your words or to see into your thoughts."

Nita tried to feel reassured. The mind, she hoped, would not fail again, and Llipel would be here to repair it if it did. "What happened after that?"

"Our time of togetherness was passing, but much remained for us to learn in this place. We stayed, but in separate places. We do not meet, not even at our ship when we fetch food. Even talk with Llare over the screen is hard for me."

"What about me?" Nita said. Llipel had revealed more about herself than she ever had before, but Nita was impatient for an answer to her earlier question. "Why am I here? Did the mind tell you to go to the cold place for me?"

Llipel pulled at the fur of her face once more; Nita was afraid that she might not reply.

"No," Llipel answered. "The screens had told me

24

that place was important, but I did not know why. I went inside; I spoke. A voice told me it was time to select, but I do not remember how I answered. I saw many receptacles along one wall, and a light under one of them went out. By a chamber bound to that receptacle by a tube, another light was shining. The voice said that a small being was now growing there, that it had to be taken from the chamber at another time. I was very frightened then. I ran from the cold room."

Llipel was tugging at her face so forcefully that Nita feared she might tear out some of her fur. She touched her guardian's arm gently. Llipel lowered her hands, then folded her arms.

"Somehow I calmed myself," Llipel said. "I questioned the screens. The mind told me that a creature was growing inside that chamber, and that I had caused this to happen. If I did not return for it, that creature would die. I told Llare of what I had done, and Llare— But I cannot speak of that." She paused. "I learned from the screens of how to care for one of your kind, and went back for you at the proper time."

"Then you—"

"Do you see why I could not tell you this before?" Llipel swatted at the air with her claws, then retracted them. "You live because of my mistake. I did not want you to know this when you were smaller and more helpless. You needed to trust me if I was to care for you."

"You didn't know," Nita said. "It wasn't your fault." Nonetheless, the story dismayed her. She had hoped there was some reason for her life; now it appeared that her existence was no more than an accident.

"I took you from the cold room. Your name is from words the voice in the cold place gave to me—it said many words, but 'Nita' was one of them, and it seemed to be a name. It was hard to care for you. You let out many cries, and some foods I gave you came out of your mouth again. I made cloths for your bottom parts from things I found in one room. I learned what foods to feed you and how to clean you in water." Llipel shuddered. "I gave you what the mind calls affection— that means, I think, a time to hold you and soothe you with my voice. Many times, I thought you might die, but you live, and I have learned. I think sometimes that is why I am here, to learn, but I do not know why."

An idea was forming in Nita's mind, one so startling that at first she could hardly accept it. "You said the cold place has many receptacles," she said slowly. "It means—" She pushed the tray of uneaten fruit away. "There may be others! You said there were more. We could bring them out, Llipel. I could have a friend."

"No!" Llipel leaned forward; her claws were out, scratching at the tiles. "We do not know their purpose, why they are there." Her usually even voice had risen. "If others are taken out, we cannot know what will come of it."

"But you said you don't remember why you came to this world. Maybe they were left here for you."

Llipel sat up straight. "That cannot be. I do not remember what was before, but the mind of my ship knew little of this world before I came here. I do not think my kind knew yours."

"But you don't know. Maybe they went to another world, and they're going to come back." Nita glanced at the mower as it floated over the grass. "Why would they leave robots here to take care of everything? Why does the mind watch over this place? Why would they leave the cafeteria to feed me? Why didn't they take the ones in the cold place with them? They must be coming back someday. They'll come back, and then—"

"Why, why. You keep saying why. You must wait for the answers to come—I see how disordered you become when answers come too soon." Llipel rose to her feet in one swift movement. "They will never return."

"Why do you say that?"

"You must not ask me why. It is not something you can know now."

"Knowing can't be worse than not knowing," Nita said.

"I try to make up for my mistake. I learn more than would have come to me without this mistake." Llipel was clearly struggling with her words now. "You bring sorrow to yourself and problems to me by hoping that your kind will come here."

"Why? Why can't I have a friend? Why do I have

to be shut up here? What'll I do if the mind fails again? If my people don't come here, I'll go and look for them. I'll—"

"Nita, there may come a time—" Llipel shook her body. "I cannot say more now."

"I'm sick of hearing about times for this and times for that! You never tell me anything I want to know! I hate you!"

Llipel gazed at her calmly, as if puzzled by this outburst. Then she turned around slowly and left the garden.

Nita was afraid to follow Llipel inside right away, even though she had little to fear from her guardian, who had always been gentle with her. Llipel had explained more to her than she ever had before, but Nita had not been satisfied with that.

Why wasn't she more like Llipel, able to accept what answers she was given and to wait until the time came for more answers? Having replies to some questions only raised others in her mind that demanded answers immediately.

She stood up, adjusted the towel around her hips, and went inside. As she hurried down the hall, Llipel suddenly emerged from the cafeteria.

Nita swallowed and looked down. "I guess I shouldn't have said I hated you."

"That is a strong word. Is the feeling as strong?"

Nita nodded. "But I don't hate you, Llipel. I was angry, that's all."

"Then the time for hate is past. I did something else for you to mark this day, but you did not let me tell it before. Come into the food room. You ask for a friend. There is a friend inside for you."

Nita trembled with anticipation as she walked toward the cafeteria and wondered what she would find. The door slid open, revealing a room filled with tables and chairs. Slots with buttons beneath them lined the walls; the recycler stood in a corner near a large screen.

She saw no one at first, then heard a soft, mewing sound. A tiny furred creature huddled under a table, next to a bowl of milk. Nita gazed into its green eyes, then crept up to it and patted its gray fur gently. It mewed again and rubbed against her leg.

"What is it?" Nita asked. "Is it a small one of your kind?" But it couldn't be, she thought. It had a tail, and thin whiskers on either side of its nose, while Llipel had no whiskers or tail. Its mouth was too wide, its face was narrower in shape, and its ears stuck out from its head instead of lying flat against it.

"It is not one of my kind. It was in another part of the cold room. A voice called it an animal subject. It was not in a chamber like yours but lay in an enclosed cell next to others of its kind. Other strange creatures are there as well."

Nita knelt next to the small animal. "Should you have taken it?"

"I questioned the voice carefully. It said that the purpose of these creatures was to see if they could live again after being taken from their cold cells. I thought there could be no harm in bringing one to you. It is called a cat."

The cat lapped at the milk. Nita sat down next to it, entranced. "Does it have a name?"

"I did not hear one."

"A cat," Nita said. The cat sprawled next to her and poked at the air with its tiny paws.

"The voice said that some of your kind lived with these creatures, but they cannot speak and think as you do. I have asked how to care for it and learned what I could before reviving it. You wanted a friend. Will you be satisfied now?"

"I think so," Nita said, trying to believe that she had a new friend at last. Llipel must have been planning this surprise for some time. She would show her guardian that she was grateful. Llipel, she supposed, only wanted what was best for her; she would try to remember that.

4

One of the west wing's doors was open. Nita had been unable to sleep and had come to the cafeteria for some food; she noticed the open door as she was about to sit down near the windows. She set down her tray and stared at the narrowing band of light until the door slid shut.

That same door had opened the day before, when she was in the garden waiting for Llipel. That day had marked the beginning of Nita's fifteenth year of life, and Llipel had gone to fetch some of Nita's favorite foods from the cafeteria. The door had closed again before Nita could reach it.

Llare must have opened it. Nita moved closer to the windows. Why was Llipel's companion hiding behind the door instead of speaking to her over the screen?

The door was opening again; Nita squinted, unable to see clearly through the darkness. Part of a head was silhouetted against the light for a moment, as though Llare had stooped to peer out, and then the light vanished. She thought of waking Llipel to ask her what Llare might be doing, but dismissed the thought. Llipel slept only every three or four nights but, when she did, was groggy if awakened too soon.

Llipel would not want her near the west wing. Her guardian had been quite firm about that yesterday during their celebration, when Nita had again begged her to allow more readings from the library or a chance to explore more of the Institute and its grounds. Llipel allowed her more freedom only grudgingly, then expected Nita to be grateful for what little she was granted. She had not shouted at her guardian so much in days, and this had been the worst of her recent outbursts.

She sat down, trying to decide what to do. She had caused Llipel enough trouble lately, with her harsh remarks and her sulking. She could not even feel sorry about that. Being calm and reasonable gained her little, since that only made Llipel think things were fine as they were. She wondered if her moods had something to do with the changes that had come to her.

"There's nothing wrong with you," Beate had told her nearly two years before. Nita was not reassured by the image's customary smile. She had been speaking to Beate more often since her body, instead of simply growing taller, had begun to change in unexpected ways.

"Are you sure?" Nita asked.

"You've read some of the biology records," Beate responded, "yet it seems you haven't understood them as well as you should have. You're starting to become a woman. That's why your breasts have started to grow, and why you've begun to bleed. This happens to all girls when they begin to mature."

"She does not have a failing in the body?" Llipel said. She was sitting on the floor of the conference room with Nita, gazing intently at the large screen.

"No. There'd be something the matter if she didn't start showing these signs soon." Beate stood up, walked around her desk, and perched near the corner. "You may feel strange, almost as if your body doesn't belong to you sometimes, but you should welcome these changes."

Nita shook back her hair. She had known changes would come, but she had not expected to feel so clumsy and disfigured when they did.

"Do you have any questions?" Beate asked.

Nita glanced at her guardian. "I see this is a new time for Nita," Llipel said to the screen. "Tell us what you can of this time."

Beate began by speaking of ovulation and went on to talk of how Nita's body was preparing her to bring young into the world. Nita was familiar with most of the terms Beate used but had never really thought of how they would apply to her.

Llipel seemed enthralled, as she always was when learning something new. "I have heard words about this before," she said, "but did not see it clearly. And this time when Earth's kind are ready for their young— is that when they came here to offer their seed?"

Beate's hazel eyes widened as she arched her brows. "Some did so, but that wasn't the only way, or even the usual fashion, in which people reproduced." She spoke then of how a man and a woman would come together.

"I see," Llipel said when Beate was finished. "I do not think this can be true of my kind, for I do not seem to have such parts in my body. Our young must enter their world in another way."

Nita wished Llipel hadn't said that. Her words made Nita feel even more uneasy with herself.

Llipel leaned forward. "And does this time come often for two of your kind to be together?"

"The time of a woman's ovulation is when she can become pregnant," Beate replied, "but that wasn't the only time people engaged in sexual acts. People also came together in this way when no children were wanted and took pleasure in the act."

Nita was appalled; if this was how her kind had reproduced themselves, she could understand why some had chosen to come to the Institute instead. "I can't believe anyone would enjoy that," she said.

"But they did," Beate said. "They enjoyed it very much, Nita. It was a way to show love and to share that love with another."

34

"Love," Llipel murmured. "It is another of your strong words."

"In fact," Beate continued, "some people had contraceptive implants so that they could share love without the possibility of a child. There is a room in the tower where such implants can be found for both men and women, so that each partner can decide when he or she is ready to become a father or mother. The screen can show you how to embed such an implant under the skin of your arm—it's really very simple."

Nita shuddered. Llipel was studying her, as if trying to see how Nita was reacting to all of this. "You do not want such closeness now," her guardian said.

Nita shook her head. "No. It wouldn't matter even if I did."

Llipel's dark eyes widened a little. "Perhaps it was not time for you to hear about all of this."

Repulsed as Nita had felt at hearing Beate's talk, she was later unable to put it out of her mind. At times, she could even long to feel the arms of one of her own people around her.

It was pointless for her to have this changing body, to feel such odd and disturbing urges. She had thought that such feelings meant that a time for togetherness was approaching, but for Llipel, togetherness seemed to mean a time for communication and companionship, not a time to share what Beate called love. Llipel had worried that the changes coming to Nita might make her ill, but Beate had put those worries to rest. Nita could not bring herself to discuss her longings with

Llipel, who would find them difficult to understand. These new feelings were another quality that made her think something was wrong with her.

She would have no young unless her people returned to the Institute. No man lived to provide her with seed; there would be no small one of her own kind to raise. Beate and Ismail had told her that not all of their people had chosen to have young. She might have become resigned to that if there had been a companion for her, someone to ease the loneliness that even her guardian and her cat could not dispel.

These thoughts had overwhelmed Nita during the celebration marking her fifteenth year. She found herself raging at Llipel for giving her life and then condemning her to this lonely existence. Llipel had watched her silently before going off to speak with Llare over a screen. Nita had grown even angrier at that. Llipel reacted that way too often lately, listening as Nita berated her, then going off for yet another conversation with Llare. Perhaps Llipel's time for togetherness with her old companion was approaching.

She stood up. Llare might be waiting for Nita to approach her first; perhaps opening the door was meant as a sign that Nita would be welcome in that wing.

She left the cafeteria and rounded the corner. Her cat was prowling in the hall near the exit; as the door opened, the animal darted into the garden just ahead of her. Nita took a breath as the door closed, wondering if Llare had seen her and was waiting.

The cat rubbed against her legs. The furry creature was a female; the screens had told her that fact. "Dusky." She crooned the name as she leaned over to scratch the cat behind the ears; Dusky often seemed as restless as she. Maybe Dusky was lonely, too.

She crept through the darkness. The sky was clear, the moon a thin crescent in the sky. Once she had shied away from entering the garden at night, had felt uneasy in a place where she could not summon light with a few words to a screen, but now she could welcome the darkness and imagine that the shadows cloaked other people.

The path's flat tiles were smooth against her bare feet. She shivered in the cool night air and wished she had put on one of the white coats or blue coveralls that were the only clothing she had ever found in the east wing. She kept near the trees along the path until she was only a few paces from the door.

"Llare?" she called out tentatively. Llare might be hoping for companionship now; she might even allow Nita to use the library in her wing.

The door began to slide open. She held her breath. As the opening widened, Dusky suddenly bounded past her and scampered toward the light. Nita leaped after the cat, stubbed her toe, and cried out harshly at the pain. The opening narrowed; Dusky ran into the hallway just before the door closed behind her.

Nita stumbled toward the door. "Llare!" she shouted as she struck the door with her fist. "Open the door! Give me back my cat!" She pounded the door again, certain that Llare could hear her. "Open this door!"

She waited, trying to calm herself. "Listen to me. I know you can understand. I won't come in if you don't want me to. Just open the door and put Dusky back outside, please." Her anger rose; Dusky was her cat, not Llare's. "Open this door!" she cried. "Give her back right now, or you'll be sorry!"

She steadied herself. Screaming at Llare would do no good. She spun around and ran back to the east wing. A small screen was just inside the door; she approached it anxiously. "I have to speak to Llare," she said. "Signal her for me—I have to ask her something."

"You are not authorized," the mind's toneless voice replied. "Llare cannot be disturbed without authorization."

"I don't care. This is important. My cat's in the west wing—I only want her back. Please let me talk to Llare."

"You have no authorization."

Nita shook her fist. The screen flickered. A face was staring out at her now, one she had never seen before. "I didn't ask for an image," she said.

"May I talk to you?" This face did not sound as calm as the other images. It had wide cheekbones, a strong chin, pale-blue eyes, and thick, disorderly light-brown hair. She could see the breadth of its shoulders under a blue coverall, and assumed that the image represented a male, although its voice was not as low as most of the men's voices were. A thin chain from which an authorization dangled was around its neck.

"Get off the screen," Nita muttered. "I have to talk to Llare."

"Llare's sleeping. Can't you talk to me?"

"But Llare can't be asleep. My cat's in the west wing. Llare must have opened the door." Why would the mind lie to her about that? She wondered if it was beginning to fail again. "What are you called, anyway?"

"My name's Sven. You're called Nita, aren't you?"

"Well, you ought to know. All the images do." Nita moved closer to the screen; the image called Sven seemed to shrink back.

"Your cat's all right," Sven said. "You don't have to worry about that. I didn't mean—"

His voice, she noticed, trembled a little. None of the faces had ever spoken to her in this manner; Sven did not sound like the mind. "I didn't ask for your image," she said. "Will you get off the screen?"

"But I'm not an image. I'm like you, except that I'm a boy. I'm real, Nita—I live here. Will you talk to me?"

She clasped her hands together, frightened, unable to believe this. "What do you mean?" she managed to say. "There's no one here except Llipel and Llare and me."

"You're wrong. I'm here, too. They just didn't want you to know, it wasn't time to know. I didn't know about you, either, until a little while ago."

Llipel had lied. No, that wasn't quite accurate. She

had kept this secret and had allowed Nita to believe that she was alone. She had said no one would come here; she had not mentioned that one of Nita's kind already dwelled in the Institute. Nita felt betrayed.

"Now you know," Sven continued. "I've been waiting for a chance to talk to you without Llare finding out." His blue eyes gazed at her intently. "I thought you'd be happy to know about me. I was excited when I found out about you."

She could not accept it. She had longed for a friend, but if Sven was real, it meant that the guardian she had always trusted had deceived her. "You can't be real," she burst out. "You're just something the mind called up. Llipel would have told me about you."

"But I can prove I'm real." His face dropped off the screen for a moment, then reappeared. He lifted his arms. Her gray cat squirmed in his grip and meowed; he drew Dusky to his chest and patted her gently.

"Dusky!" she cried.

"I would have put her back in the garden right away, but you sounded so angry—I didn't know what you might do. I'll show you I'm real. You can come and meet me, in the tower. We can talk in the lobby—I've never seen that room before. Will you come?"

"But I can't. I'm not authorized to go there."

"I'm authorized. I can ask the doors to open for you."

She hesitated. The boy might be real, unbelievable as that seemed, but she didn't know anything about him. He might not let her leave the tower again. He was authorized, while she wasn't.

"I'll come there," she said at last, "but I'll find another way to get to the tower." An idea occurred to her. "Llipel's asleep. I might be able to take her authorization."

Sven nodded. "I'll wait for you, then. I'll bring your cat there, too."

The screen went blank.

5

Llipel and she always slept in the room marked AD-MINISTRATOR, DEPARTMENT OF EMBRYOLOGY, Nita on the couch, Llipel curled up on the desk. "Keep the light dim," Nita whispered to the screen near the door, although even bright light was unlikely to wake her guardian. She hesitated in front of the door, then pressed her hand against it.

The door opened; she stepped inside. For a moment, she thought of waking her guardian and asking her what to do. Llipel might have had reasons for concealing Sven's existence from her. But Sven would be expecting her to come to the tower alone.

Llipel was still deeply asleep; her thin arms were wrapped around her long legs. Nita crept across the pale carpet and stopped in front of the desk.

She was still numb with the shock of finding out about Sven; now she was planning to steal from her guardian. Llipel's unlidded eyes were covered by their pearly membranes; when she slept, little could rouse her. She tiptoed around the desk until she was behind Llipel, who was lying on her side.

The chain was barely visible under her neck fur. Nita would have to ease it over her head somehow. She reached toward the chain, then noticed that a thin, flat piece of metal joined the links in the back. She touched that part of the chain and tugged a little as her fingers gripped it tightly. The two ends suddenly separated; the authorization slid down and clinked as the thin rectangle struck the top of the desk.

She froze. Llipel whistled softly, but did not move. Nita crept around the desk. The authorization was lying near Llipel's left shoulder; she picked it up.

Her heart pounded; her throat was dry as she fled from the room. She was several paces down the hall before she halted to study the chain. The thin piece of metal, it seemed, was a clasp; she put the ends of the chain together and hung it around her neck.

Pangs of guilt pricked her for only a second. If Llipel had told her the truth earlier, she would not have had to take the chain. A time for togetherness with one of her own people had finally come.

Inside a closet, in a room called INSTITUTE PERSON-NEL ONLY, she found a pair of coveralls that would fit her if she rolled up the arms and legs. She almost never wore clothes and might be concealing little that Sven had not already seen. But the images on the screen had always been clothed, and Beate had told her that her people removed their garments when they wanted to share love. She did not want Sven to think she wanted that much togetherness.

At the end of the hall, perpendicular to the south exit, stood the wide door marked GENETICS DEPART-MENT. She stepped forward, fearing that the door might not open after all. But she had authorization now; the scanner would have to let her pass. Her hand touched the door; it slid open.

She had seen diagrams of the Institute and knew that a hallway leading to the tower lay beyond the door. The ceiling's light panels flowed on, one after another, until a band of illumination stretched to the far end of the hall. Her bare feet padded along the smooth gray floor, carrying her past pale walls and closed doors. When she reached the end of the corridor, she hesitated for a moment, took a breath, then touched the door.

She stepped forward as the door slid past her. The tower's lobby was larger than any room she had ever seen, its ceiling so high overhead that she felt disoriented. A glass booth stood at her right; panels marked with bright splashes of color were on the far wall, above a long, cushioned platform that resembled a couch.

Sven was sitting on a square platform near the front doors. She walked toward him slowly, almost expecting him to disappear as the images did when she was through talking to them. His lips curved up as she came nearer, but his smile seemed more uncertain than those of the screen images.

"Hello," she said, unable to think of anything else to say.

"Greetings," he replied.

She studied the boy. The sleeves of his blue coverall were rolled up to his elbows. His arms were thicker and more muscular than hers, and although he was seated, she was sure he was taller as well. His blue eyes were large; his skin seemed paler than it had on the screen and was much lighter than her own dark-brown skin.

She reached out and touched his arm; he started. "You *are* real," she said.

He nodded. His unevenly trimmed hair was much shorter than her own. "I'm glad you got here. I didn't know if you would." His throat moved as he swallowed. "I thought you might be afraid to come."

"I was."

The boy was staring at her. When she met his eyes, he looked away hastily. "Uh, I brought your cat," he said. "You can see for yourself." He pointed behind himself with one arm.

She walked around the platform. Dusky was curled up on the floor, asleep, but another animal was near her, a large cat with thick orange fur. She looked up at Sven. "You have a cat, too?"

"His name's Tanj. It's short for Tangerine—his fur

has the same kind of color. Llare got him from the cryonic facility for me."

"My cat came from the cold place, too." She leaned against the platform. In all her imaginings about a possible encounter with someone like herself, she had never expected to feel so uneasy. There was so much that she wanted to say, yet she could not bring herself to speak the words.

"I had to take Llipel's authorization while she was sleeping," she said at last, although he already knew what she had planned to do. "How did you get authorized?"

"The same way—I took this when Llare was asleep." He gestured at his authorization. "I've taken it a few times. That's how I found out about you. I wanted to talk to you as soon as I knew, and then I wondered if you'd want to talk to me."

"But why would you think I wouldn't want to see you?" she asked as she leaned toward him. "I always hoped I'd see someone like me, that our people might come back here, that I'd have a friend." She held out her hand; he shrank away. She wondered if she had said something wrong. "You wanted me to come here, Sven, but now you don't seem that happy to see me."

He shook his head. "I am. It's just—" He paused. "Llipel probably didn't let you find out certain things, but I had the library. Most of what's there is about the Institute, but I found books and tapes that showed other things. Our kind—they were cruel in a lot of

46

ways. You probably don't know how cruel. Sometimes I wish I'd never found out."

"Llare let you use the library?" She felt a stab of envy.

"He didn't for a long time, but I kept after him about it. Maybe he just got tired of hearing me complain. Finally, he said that maybe the time had come for me to learn more about my kind, but he didn't seem happy about it."

"He?"

Sven shrugged. "Llare said words like 'he' or 'she' don't really apply to him or Llipel. It's just easier to think of them as one thing or the other. It makes them seem more like us, I suppose." He ran a hand through his thick light-brown hair. "They're not like our kind, though. For one thing, they're gentler."

Sven was right about that; Nita thought of her own outbursts and displays of temper. She could understand Sven's feelings. He had undoubtedly compared himself to his guardian and worried about why he could not maintain such calm himself. But why would he say that their people were cruel?

"Once I was happy about what I was," he continued. "Not about everything, but I thought I'd change when I was older. I knew my people built this place not just to store embryos and animals but to find ways to prolong life and postpone death for their kind. Llare doesn't think about death—maybe his kind lives longer than ours—but our people feared it."

"I know that," she said. "I learned a few things from the screens." Her people weakened as they aged and sometimes succumbed to various illnesses. She could not recall ever being ill and almost could not imagine it.

"This Institute was built to help people," Sven said. "I told myself that people like that wouldn't have forgotten us, that they might come back someday. They did other things, too—they studied the planets and stars, they created intelligences like the mind—they did so much. I used to think of how happy they must have been, to have other people to live with and learn from and help. But when I found out what they were really like, I began to think it'd be better if I left this place and never came back."

"You mustn't say that." She was about to stretch her hand out to him once more, but drew back. "Anyway, if you left, our guardians would probably go after you in their ship. You don't know what's out there, and they'd be afraid for you." Another thought came to her. "Llipel and Llare aren't authorized now," she said. "They'll be wondering about us when they wake up."

"It's all right. I told the mind to let them know where we are and to let them use the screens to talk to each other. We can go back before they get too worried."

She looked down. "Llipel's going to be concerned, anyway," she said. "When I go back, she may not let me see you again." She longed to ask him more about what he had read that disturbed him so much, but talking about it only seemed to make him more unhappy. He seemed to want a friend, but shied away from her at the same time. Had he changed his mind? Did he regret having asked her to come here?

He slipped down from the platform, then beckoned to her. "There's something you should see. I found it while I was waiting for you. I guess I should show you now."

He led her toward the glass booth, which was near the back of the lobby, not far from where she had entered. Behind the booth stood doors with rows of numbers above each; those had to be the lifts that could carry one to the upper floors of the tower. A small hallway between two of the lift doors led to an exit. She called up her memory of the diagrams she had seen; that door would lead into the garden.

Three desks and four chairs were inside the booth, which was open on one side. Sven went to one of the desks and pulled out a drawer. "Look."

She peered into the drawer and saw several flat rectangles and circular disks that were attached to chains. "More authorizations!" she cried out.

"Now you know why they never let us in here." He removed two authorizations, then closed the drawer. "They could have given them to us before. Now we can have our own." He handed one of the chains to her, then thrust the other into his side pocket.

She hung the second authorization around her neck, then followed him out of the booth. She was authorized now, and she would have a friend; everything would be different. Whatever Sven's darker thoughts were, he would surely be cheered by that fact. She wanted to reach out to him then and see her happiness reflected in his eyes.

"I wish I'd known about you before," she said as she moved closer to him; he took a step back. "I know we'll be friends. We will, won't we? I wanted a friend for so long, and now you're here. I knew my time for separateness was passing, and you must have felt it, too. Maybe our people aren't here because it wasn't our time for togetherness, and maybe they'll return now that it is."

He shook his head. "They'll never return."

"How do you know?"

"I know more about them than you do."

"If you tell me what you found out, maybe it won't seem so bad, whatever it is. I'm not like Llare or Llipel—I'm like you. I'd understand. You should tell me what you know. Aren't friends supposed to talk to each other?"

"You might not want to find out what I know," he replied.

"What's the matter? You wanted to talk to me, didn't you?"

"Maybe I shouldn't have."

A sadder look had come into his face. She was suddenly annoyed with him and hurt by the way he seemed to be withdrawing from her already. "I'm authorized now," she said. "I can find out anything you know. Why did you even talk to me over the screen if you were going to act like this? You said you were excited when you found out about me, but you don't seem very happy now. You asked me to come here. Maybe you shouldn't have bothered if it's going to be like this."

He lifted his chin. "Maybe not."

"I wish you hadn't now!" Her voice was rising. "But you're the only one like me here, so I guess I'm stuck with you!"

"Nita—" He spun around then and strode toward one of the lifts. Before she could call out an apology, the door had closed behind him.

6

The numerals above the lift door lit up one by one until the last winked out. Sven had gone to the fifteenth floor. Rather than trying to cheer him, she had driven him away with harsh words. Maybe she should have asked the screens about how to behave with one of her own people.

Llipel had not told her about Sven. Now she wondered if her guardian might have been justified in keeping that secret. The boy had said that his kind, and Nita's, were cruel; perhaps Llipel and Llare had wanted to shield them both from that cruelty. The screen images did not seem unkind, but then they weren't really people at all, only images stored in the mind's memory. The real people might have been different. Maybe a time for togetherness came only rarely to her people, as it apparently did for Llare and Llipel.

Nita turned away from the lift and walked toward the front doors; two images on the wall to her left suddenly caught her eye. Unlike those of the screens, these two faces did not move or speak. Metal plates under the images held lettering, but she would have recognized the faces even without seeing their names.

"Kwalung Chun," she read aloud. "Ferdinand Ibarra." The tilted eyes of Kwalung and the brown ones of Ibarra gazed into the distance. What had happened to them? What had happened to the others who had worked here with them?

They had founded the Institute. Others had labored here with them, had preserved embryos of their kind for some purpose. They had studied the workings of bodies, seeking ways to strengthen and heal them. They had wanted to prolong life and to bring new life into the world. Was that the work of cruel people?

She walked on. Beyond the transparent doors, the sky was lightening a little. A flat surface stretched toward the dark mass of the forest that surrounded the Institute. She imagined a ship landing there and her own people stepping from it. Sven might be mistaken in saying that no one would return for them; perhaps he didn't know as much as he claimed.

If she could not reach out to Sven, she might be unable to reach out to others. Her people might not want her then. Sven was like her; she should be able to sympathize with him. If she had found out about him first, would she have approached him easily, or would she have been wary? If she had asked him to come here, would she have disappointed him somehow? He had believed himself to be alone here with their guardians; maybe he saw her as an intruder. Perhaps dreams about encounters with their people, thoughts of smiling faces, welcoming arms, and an instant empathy and joy, had not prepared either of them for an actual meeting.

She would have to go to Sven or retreat to the east wing for good. She could not let their meeting end this way.

She walked back to the lifts. One door opened as her authorization was scanned; she stepped inside uncertainly. The door slid shut; she waited.

"To which floor do you wish to go?" a voice asked.

"Fifteen." She felt a brief moment of heaviness, then nothing, and wondered if the lift was moving. It might break down and trap her between floors; her mouth grew dry at the thought. Her life depended on the Institute's artificial intelligence and the technology that served it, and the mind had begun to fail before. Someday the lights might not shine so readily; the cafeteria's slots might not be filled with food by the synthesizer. She might have to leave the Institute then, and she had no idea of how to survive. Even Llipel and her ship might be of little help to her. That was another reason to reach out to the boy; she and Sven might have to depend on each other someday.

The door opened. The lobby had disappeared; she gazed into a large room that seemed to be another cafeteria. A red carpet covered the floor; the glass-topped tables had silvery metal legs, while the chairs were covered with red cushioning. Slots lined the wall to her left.

Sven was sitting at a table near the room's wide windows. He lifted his head as she approached. "I didn't think you'd follow me," he said.

"The lift scared me a little," she admitted.

"There's a stairway, you know." He looked away. "I was going to come down to the lobby, and then I was afraid you might have left."

She sat down across from him. "I didn't mean to say what I did."

He kept his eyes lowered, refusing to look at her. "When I saw you," he said, "all these feelings came to me. I was glad, but I was afraid, too. I thought—" He raised his head. "I wanted to say everything to you I could, all at once, and then I was afraid to say anything at all."

"I felt the same way." She leaned back in her chair. "What I don't understand is why Llipel and Llare didn't tell us about each other."

Sven rubbed at the tabletop with one finger. "They don't think the way we do. I notice that more now. You'd think they'd seem more familiar, but Llare seems stranger instead. They came here from somewhere else, they can't eat our food, they don't look like us, and they don't see things the way we do."

"They might have thought it wasn't a time for us to be together," she said, "but they still could have told us. We could have spoken to each other over the screens, even if it wasn't a time to meet."

He frowned. "I've been in the library. I know what our people were like. Llare knows—he can't read, but he could listen and watch some of the visual records. I think he was afraid of what we might do if we met."

She thought of the time Beate had explained sex to her and to Llipel. Had their guardians feared that she and Sven might perform such acts, and that a child might result from them? But she could not have had a child before her body began to change, and the implants Beate had mentioned could prevent a pregnancy.

Sven was a boy; could that get in the way of their becoming friends? She did not see how; surely they could still be companions. Whenever she had imagined meeting those of her own kind, she had seen faces and bodies as varied as the ones the screen showed, but it hadn't seemed to matter whether they were women or men. They would, after all, be people. Sven was like her; he was probably as puzzled by their kind's way of showing love as she was.

Thinking of this was not making her any more comfortable in the boy's presence. "It sounds strange to hear you call Llare a 'he,' " she said quickly. "I always thought of Llipel and Llare as females."

"Why?"

"Maybe because Llipel's more like the female images than the male ones. Her voice is more like theirs."

"I think of Llare as a male," he said, "but that's probably because I'm one myself. I used to think that, when I was older, I'd be more like him. I told myself that we were both intelligent beings, so we should think the same way, but—" He was silent for a moment. "He's always been kind, in his own way. I don't think his people would have done the things ours did."

"Why do you keep saying those things about our kind?"

He rested his arms on the table. "The library has records about some things our people did. Llare didn't want me to see them, but he knew about them. I think I know why this Institute was started."

"But so do I," she said. "To do research, to store embryos until—"

"Why hasn't anyone come back for them?" he asked.

"Well, I used to think that they'd gone to another world, but that they were going to come back someday. Then I thought that they might have forgotten about us." That possibility was disturbing to consider, but less painful than believing that they might remember and did not care.

Sven shook his head. "They haven't forgotten, and they won't come back. I think they're all dead, that we're the only ones left."

His words shocked her. "But why?"

"Are you sure you really want to know?"

"You can tell me," she forced herself to reply. "We don't have to have secrets, Sven. It doesn't have to be like—" Llipel had hidden too much from her; she had to have known about Sven. Now she wondered if she could trust Llipel again.

"You'd find out, anyway, if you went to the library. But maybe it'll be easier if I tell you. They had wars, Nita." His eyes narrowed. "But you don't know what a war is, do you?" He did not wait for a reply. "It's when one group of people got together and tried to kill as many of another group as they could. They had lots of ways to do it, ways I don't really understand, weapons that could destroy every living thing and make it impossible to survive on the land where they were used. Then they'd build other weapons, ones that could protect them against the ones they already had. Even when they weren't fighting, they seemed to believe that another war would come sooner or later."

Her throat tightened; she could hardly believe what she was hearing. "Why would they do such things?"

"Oh, they had reasons. One group had something another group wanted, or believed something another group didn't agree with. Or they just hated each other."

"But how could they treat their own kind that way?"

"They did," Sven replied. "They'd fight, and then they'd stop fighting for a while and make agreements, but those agreements didn't last. All of them knew that if they couldn't control themselves, they might destroy everything, and sometimes they didn't use all the weapons they had. They'd hold some back as a threat, hoping they'd never have to do anything with them. But in the end, I think they used them all."

She felt stunned, wanting to deny his words. "Look at this place," she said desperately. "How could people like that have built it and worked here together? The ones who came here must have been able to get along."

"Oh, they could be cooperative," Sven said. "They had to be to work together to make the weapons they did, to get a group together for a war."

He turned toward the window; his throat moved as he swallowed. "Llare told me about times for togetherness," he continued, "and times for separateness. He said he didn't know why he and Llipel were here, only that they seemed compelled to be. Our kind must have had times for peace and times for war. I don't suppose they could have helped it any more than Llare can stop being what he is. He knew what our kind was— no wonder he and Llipel didn't want us to meet. They probably thought our time for fighting would come."

It couldn't be true; she refused to believe it. She thought of the times she had been angry; didn't they always pass, and wasn't she able to control them some of the time? Or would the violent feelings overtake her eventually, robbing her of her will?

"I think I know why those embryos were stored," Sven said. "Someone must have known that a war that could destroy everything might come, and wanted to be sure some people had a chance to survive. This Institute was made to last for a long time. They probably hoped survivors would come here, find the embryos, and start all over again. But there weren't any survivors, and no one to come for us except Llare and

Llipel. We shouldn't have been revived at all. Maybe it's a good thing no one will come for the others."

Nita bowed her head, horrified at her people's deeds. She understood Sven's moodiness now, and the shame and despair he must have felt when he first learned about what their people had done. She longed to reassure him, but what could she say?

"Did the library tell you all of this?" she managed to ask.

"It didn't say that was why the Institute was built, but I could figure that out from the records, once I knew about wars. The mind doesn't remember much about the last war, only that it came just before it lost contact with everything outside. Our people had a lot of reasons for their wars, reasons for making them seem necessary. They had fine-sounding reasons for the Institute, too—probably didn't want to admit the real ones. They were like that—saying things they didn't mean or that weren't true, breaking promises, hiding their real feelings with talk."

The sky was growing lighter. She stood up and walked unsteadily to the windows. The Institute's east and west wings stretched toward the windowless expanse that held the cold place; the garden was below. A forest surrounded the structure, which was bordered by a grassy space kept trimmed by the mowers and weeded by the gardeners. A wall surrounded a large courtyard next to the west wing; with its flowers and shrubs, the courtyard was another garden.

In the moments before dawn, the forest seemed

peaceful. The creatures that lived there were free of her kind now.

She thought then of the first time Dusky had killed a bird in the garden. She had cried even after Ismail explained that cats had such instincts, could not act in any other way; the instincts ran too deep. Her kind had killed other animals for food, but Nita had assumed, from what Ismail told her, that material synthesizers such as the one in the cafeteria had freed them of that need.

She could understand killing animals for food, cruel as it seemed, if there was no other way to survive. Even Llipel had speculated that her own kind might once have done so and that her sharp claws might be a relic of such a time. But wars could not have had such a purpose. Her people had feared death, yet had risked it to bring death to others.

She made her way back to the table. "Why did they do it?" she said as she sank into her chair. "Why?"

"Maybe they couldn't help themselves. Wars meant a lot to them. They set down a lot of writings about wars. The library doesn't have many of them, but some of the records listed others. They wrote about courage and bravery and winning and warriors—people who made wars—as if they were wonderful things. Sometimes they set down arguments against wars, but that was probably when it wasn't their time for fighting."

"We mustn't fight," she said. "We can think, we can know what fighting brings. We don't have to be like that."

"Maybe we won't have any choice," he responded. "That time might come when we're older."

"No. I won't let it." She clung to that hope, however futile it was. "Maybe you shouldn't have gone to the library. If we didn't know this—"

"It's better to know. This way, we'll know what's happening to us if that time ever comes, and maybe we can do something about it."

"We could stay separated." She nearly choked on the words. Had she found one of her people only to be separated from him again? "We couldn't fight, then."

Sven raised his head. "I thought of that. I worried about whether I should talk to you at all, but then I convinced myself it was our time to meet. I told myself that you should know what I do, that it wasn't right to keep it to myself, and that you might discover it for yourself, anyway, later. But now—" He brushed back his hair awkwardly with one hand. "You looked so happy in the lobby when you were saying we'd be friends, before you got angry with me. I wanted to feel the same way, the way I would have felt about meeting you if I hadn't found out all these things. I don't want to be like our people were. I keep telling myself that I'm not like them, and then I think of what they did."

"I used to think there was something wrong with me," Nita said. "I thought it was only because I wasn't more like Llipel. Sven, what can we do?"

"I don't know." His cheeks reddened. "Whatever happens, I'd be sorry if I couldn't see you again."

"So would I." She reached across the table and took his hand. His fingers were longer, his palm broader, but his was a hand like her own, without fur and claws. Behind his eyes, there was a mind like hers. What their people had done, however horrible, was past; she would do everything in her power to see that their deeds did not touch her and the boy. "We can be friends, at least for now. We can, can't we? I promise you I'll be a friend. Please promise me that you won't be so unhappy, that you'll be glad we're together, whatever comes."

He did not speak. The sorrowful look that had angered and hurt her before moved her now. She squeezed Sven's hand; she had thought that touching one of her own kind would not be too different from touching Llipel, but she could feel a warmth rushing through her.

Sven looked up and smiled. She seemed to feel his smile from the inside as she smiled back.

He slipped his hand from hers. She wondered if she had been holding it too tightly. She would have to question Beate and Ismail about more of their customs; she did not know how to behave with one of her own kind.

"I am glad I found out about you, Nita," he said. "I'm not sorry about that, but you did scare me a little, shouting in the garden and then again in the lobby. I thought maybe it was your time for fighting."

She giggled. "It isn't, really. I shout so much at Llipel sometimes—she'd tell you that it's just the way

I am. Maybe I wouldn't do it so often if she'd show more of a reaction, but it never seems to affect her that much."

"I know what you mean. With Llare, I'd just get quiet and refuse to talk, but he'd decide then that maybe it was a time of silence, or something."

"One thing puzzles me," she said. "I go into the garden a lot, and the west wing has windows facing it. You could have seen me there any number of times and I wouldn't have known you were there. Why did it take you so long to find out about me?"

"Llare didn't let me into the rooms on that side, except for the bathrooms, and later, the library, and they don't have windows. He wouldn't authorize me to enter the others, and I had the courtyard when I wanted to go outside. I knew about the garden, but he told me Llipel went there and that it wasn't a time of togetherness for her."

"Then how did you finally find out?"

"I took Llare's authorization one night," Sven said. "I knew more about how the mind functioned by then, so I gave it an order to allow me inside all the west wing's rooms, even when I wasn't authorized. Llare never found out, so he never overrode my command. I made sure I didn't go into those rooms unless he was out by his ship. That's how I first saw you, in the garden."

She was struck by his enterprise, and a little annoyed that she hadn't thought of taking Llipel's authorization earlier. She had berated her guardian and

64

begged for more freedom instead of acting for herself.

"What did you do then?" she asked.

"I was so shocked I didn't know what to do. I didn't know how you'd react, and there was a chance you knew about me already and just didn't want to meet me. I took Llare's authorization three times after that, and sometimes I saw you in the garden when he was out by his ship, but Llipel was usually with you."

He had certainly seen her naked; she wore clothes only when the air in the garden was cool. She wondered what Sven looked like without his clothes; she knew his body would be different from hers. It was odd to think of garments as something to hide behind rather than as coverings to protect her from the cold.

"I had to find out if it was a time for togetherness," Sven continued. "I almost called out to you once, and then I heard you talking to Llipel in the garden about being alone, wanting a friend like yourself. I knew I'd have to meet you then."

Nita realized that she could not predict what the coming days would bring. Sven was something indeterminate, someone whose actions she could not foresee. She trembled slightly, feeling both anticipation and fear.

"I wish we could stay here for a while," she said, "but we should go back to our guardians. They're probably worrying about us by now if they're awake. Without their authorizations, they can't even call us over the screens."

"You're right. But don't give up your authorization.

65

We know their secret now, and we ought to be able to meet when we like. Tell me you'll meet me again soon."

"Of course I will." She averted her eyes as they stood up. Sven lingered near his chair for a moment, as if reluctant to leave, then walked with her toward the lift.

The two cats were prowling the lobby. They bounded toward Nita and Sven as they left the lift. The boy picked up Tanj; Nita followed him with her cat toward the door that led into the garden. Another door, near the exit, was marked SECURITY. She had seen that room on diagrams but had never been told what it contained; the word seemed oddly ominous now as she thought of what Sven had told her about their people.

Nita set Dusky down near a bush. "I'll talk to you later over the screen," Sven said. "Remember—don't give up your authorization."

"I won't. I'll tell Llipel it's our time for togetherness. She'll have to understand that."

The orange cat squirmed in the boy's arms. Sven began to walk toward the west wing, then looked back. "If they kept this a secret, they may have other secrets, too. I'm beginning to wonder how much they might have kept from us."

She nodded, not wanting to think of that now.

7

Llipel was tugging at the fur around her mouth as she paced in the hall near the cafeteria. She stiffened when Nita approached her.

"You are here," Llipel said. She lowered her arms and stopped pacing. "I am most curious."

"Did you talk to Llare?"

"That was my first action. The screen allowed me to speak to Llare. We were told where you were." Llipel was slurring her words a bit more than usual.

"I had to go," Nita said. "Sven spoke to me over the screen and asked me to meet him in the tower. You knew about him, didn't you? You were authorized— you had to know."

"I knew."

"He and I are both authorized now, and we're going

x

67

to stay that way, but we brought back the authorizations we took from you and Llare."

Llipel tilted her head a little. Nita pulled one of the chains over her head, then moved toward her guardian, holding out the authorization. Llipel suddenly raised her arms and held her hands in front of her chest, claws out.

She's frightened, Nita thought, and then: She's scared of me now. The defensive gesture dismayed her.

"What has taken place with the boy?" Llipel asked.

"I was in the garden with Dusky, and then a door in the west wing opened and she ran inside. I went after her, and then the door closed, so I came back here and tried to call Llare over the screen. That's when I saw Sven's image. He asked me to meet him in the tower."

"So you went there alone."

"Maybe I shouldn't have taken your authorization, but I had to see him. I didn't want to wake you, and I was afraid you wouldn't let me go."

"And what came after that?"

"We talked," Nita said. "He told me how he learned about me and what he's found out in the library. We want to be friends, Llipel. It must be a time of togetherness for us now."

Llipel retracted her claws. Nita stepped toward her and handed her the chain. Llipel hung it around her neck while watching Nita warily. "I knew that a time would come for you to know of Sven. I did not think—"

"But why didn't you tell me before? Why did you keep it a secret?"

Llipel leaned against the wall. "I should not have gone to the cold room. I could not say to you that Llare had revived the boy only a short time before I went there. Llare was frightened and did not tell me of that error until I had made the same mistake with you. Our time of separateness was upon us then, and we did not often speak. It took much for Llare to tell me of the deed, and much for me to tell Llare of what I had done." Llipel adjusted the chain. "I could tell you of my own mistake, but not Llare's, not as long as Llare would not allow me to tell of it. I promised— no. I do not think your people have a word for it. It is a kind of pledge, but more than that. It is saying one will not speak of a thing and then entering a time of silence about it."

How many other secrets had Llipel promised to keep? Nita walked past her guardian and entered the cafeteria. The fruit juice, bread, and cheese she had taken from a slot earlier still sat on the table near the window where she had left them. She walked toward the table, picked up the food, and dumped it into the recycler's round opening; she had lost her appetite.

Llipel had followed her into the room. Nita sank into a chair; her guardian sat down on the floor near her. "Is that the only reason you didn't tell me," Nita said, "that you made a kind of promise to Llare that you wouldn't say anything about Sven?"

"That came later, what you call a promise. We brought

you out to care for you, but our own time of separateness had come. Llare took you both for a time,
and then I would bring you here, but there was much
trouble in caring for one, and more with two. We learned
it would be easier if each of us cared for one of you."

Nita could understand that; the screens had told her
of how long her kind remained helpless and dependent
when young. "But when we were older," she said,
"when we could do some things for ourselves—couldn't
you have told us then?"

"The screens said that young ones of your kind might
be brought together for play and learning. It was strange
to hear that, for I felt a need for my separateness and
a time to hear only my own thoughts. But you were
not of my kind, so I did not know your needs. When
you came to say words, to crawl and stand and walk
a little, Llare would leave the boy with me for a time,
or I would take you to Llare. Sometimes you played,
and other days you stayed apart, but then a day came
when the boy struck you and hurt you before I could
stop it. I feared that you were harmed."

Nita thought of what Sven had told her. Did their
violent time come upon them so soon, even before they
were fully grown?

"I told Llare of what Sven had done," Llipel continued. "We agreed that it was not your time of togetherness, whatever the mind said. We knew also
that—" She fell silent for a moment. "We did not want
either of you harmed by the other. It was best to keep
you apart after that."

70

"Sven told me what he learned about our people."
Her throat tightened. "I suppose you already know
what he's found out. He told me how they fought, how
one group would kill another, about their weapons."

"We knew," Llipel responded. "We hoped that this
time would not come for you, because the mind said
that your kind had times without fighting. But we soon
saw our mistake. We kept you apart, and then learned
that you were in a time of forgetfulness—you had no
memory of your togetherness."

"That isn't quite true," Nita said. "I think I did recall
something, but I used to think I had only imagined it.
I had a faint memory of another like me."

"Llare and I agreed that you would not know of each
other until we saw what changes came to you later.
We entered our time of silence." She looked up at Nita
solemnly. "We wanted to be sure a time of not-fighting
was near before you learned of each other."

Was Llipel being completely honest with her now?
Maybe she had intended to keep the secret for good,
and was only saying this because Nita now knew about
Sven. "You knew I longed for a friend," she said. "Didn't
that tell you that it might be time for me to have one?"

Llipel whistled softly, then mewed a protest. "That
feeling passed from you—it was not always in you,
and your body did not fail from that longing. You seemed
content with the companionship of the cat. That told
me it was not yet your time of togetherness."

Nita said, "That time has come."

"It seems so, if you are moved to take my author-

71

ization from me and run to that boy." Llipel waved an arm. "I sensed that this time was near. Llare told me of how restless Sven was growing, of how often he searched the library's records. We would have told you of each other before long." She gazed at Nita steadily with her black eyes. "Now you have found each other, and I fear for you."

"There's nothing to fear." Nita hoped that was true. "We want to be friends—we won't harm each other. We may be the only ones of our kind left—we have to be friends."

Llipel did not reply.

8

Nita had viewed the library through a screen before going there, but the room was smaller than she had expected. Tables, couches, and chairs were grouped in the center of the room, while slots that resembled those in the cafeteria covered the walls.

Sven was expecting her; he looked up as she walked toward him. He was sitting on a couch and held a flat reading screen on his lap. Llare was seated on the floor near him, but before Nita could speak, Sven's guardian stood up, murmured a greeting, then glided from the room.

"Llare could have stayed," Nita said. Llare's presence might have eased the awkwardness she now felt.

"It's all right. He thought we might want to be by ourselves. He usually goes out to the courtyard in the

73

afternoon, so maybe we can talk to him then." He pointed toward a desk to her left on which a small console sat. "That's the catalogue. I'll show you how it works. You ask it for records on a subject, and if it isn't sure what you want, it'll ask you some questions until it finds out. Then it searches the records and displays them on a screen. You don't really have to come here to use the library, now that you've got that." He gestured at the authorization around her neck. "But I like coming here to read, anyway."

"I should have brought a reading screen with me," she said. "I didn't think—"

"Turn around. See those thin slots on either side of the door? Just press a button under one of them."

She went toward the door and pushed a button; the slot extruded a flat screen. She pulled it out, walked back to the boy, and sat down on the couch across from him.

Sven looked different. His thick light-brown hair was now curled around his ears and was shorter and more even around his face and neck. She wished that she had trimmed her own hair, which had grown past her shoulders; she had never worried about how she looked before. He wore a blue coverall, but this one fit him more snugly than the one he had worn in the tower. She suddenly wished that she had something to wear besides blue coveralls and white coats; the images on the screen often appeared in a variety of garments.

Sven's face reddened a little; she realized that she

was staring at him. "Look directly at a person when you meet," Beate had told her, "but don't stare in a way that might make that person uncomfortable." Nita was having a hard time grasping the distinction. Beate and Ismail had also demonstrated such gestures as shaking hands and taking a person lightly by the arms before planting a kiss on one cheek, both of which had apparently been customary greetings.

"Well, what do you want to look at first?" he asked.

"I don't know where to start."

"How much reading have you done?"

"I've read some things about the Institute's work, and writings about plants and animals. I know some astronomy and a little about medicine. I wasn't allowed to read a lot of things."

"It'll be hard at first," he said, "depending on what you pick. You'll see unfamiliar words, but the reading gets easier the more you do of it."

"You never told me what Llare said when you came back from the tower."

"He said he would have told me about you soon, but he seemed interested in how I discovered it for myself. I kept thinking he'd scold me, but he didn't. I wish I could believe him. I wonder if he would have said anything if I hadn't found it out."

She understood what he meant; knowing about Sven seemed to increase the barriers between her and her own guardian. "I used to wonder," she said, "how Llipel could stay with me when she had to be apart from Llare. She thought it was because I wasn't one of her kind, that she didn't have the same feeling with me, the same need to stay apart."

"Llare told me that, too. He said the feeling was very strong, almost like a command—that it wasn't time to be with Llipel, that he had to look at everything through his own eyes and not hers. That's how he described it."

"Llipel said it was like having to hear everything through her own ears."

"And yet they could still speak over the screens," Sven said. "Maybe that was mostly about us, maybe that's why they talked then. They can still talk to each other, even during separateness." He frowned. "That's probably more than you can say for our kind. When they had wars, all they must have thought about was killing and winning. They even thought about it some-times during their times for peace."

"Please. You don't have to think of that now."

Sven put his screen aside. "When I first found out about our people, when I realized what they were like, I told myself I was glad I was alone, that there weren't any others like me. Then I found out about you, and all these feelings came that frightened me. I was happy, but I was angry with Llare for never telling me—I don't think I was ever so angry before. I couldn't say anything to him, and then I wondered if he was trying to protect us. Now I worry that I might really hurt you someday. I hurt you once—Llare told me about that."

"But you didn't know any better."

"Does that make it all right?" He cleared his throat. "We might hurt Llare and Llipel. Have you thought of that? Maybe when our violent time comes, we'll go after them."

Nita tried to smile. "That wouldn't be easy. I wouldn't want to get in the way of their claws." She studied the boy, trying not to stare at him this time. Somehow she could not imagine him being deliberately cruel, whatever their people had been like.

Sven shifted on his couch. "You know, I've never seen Llare use his claws for anything except grooming himself and me, or poking at something, or combing my cat when Tanj lets him, which isn't often. I don't think they know anything about fighting." He shook his head. "There's another thing. Now that we've met, and we're older, they might leave. They have a ship, and this isn't their world. It might be like their time of separateness—they might feel that the time's come to leave."

Nita was silent. What purpose would there be to her life then? Llipel had taken pleasure in her companionship and in guiding her. Nita's existence might be the result of her guardian's mistake, but Llipel had clearly taken a bit of joy in raising her. Each was separated from others of her own kind, but their companionship had eased that loss a little. She could know that her existence had given Llipel some solace.

But what would happen if Llipel and Llare left the Institute? She and Sven would have no purpose. They would learn what they could from the library, knowledge that had no goal except passing the time until death. They might leave this place, but would find no other people. They might have closeness that would end in a fight. They could go to the cold place and revive other companions, but if others like them lived, they might only bring more death to this world.

"Maybe we're the ones who'll have to leave the Institute," she said. "I'd do that before I'd hurt Llipel, whatever secrets she's kept." Her own impatience and growing distrust might push her into acting against her guardian; perhaps suspicion and fear were the first signs of her kind's violent time.

Sven stood up. "Come on. I should show you how the catalogue works."

She shook her head. "I want to see some of what you found—about the wars and what our people did. You can show it to me now."

"Are you sure you're ready for that?"

"If I see the worst about our people and get it over with, I'll be prepared for anything else. Maybe it's better to see it instead of imagining all kinds of things."

"If that's what you want." He picked up his screen and sat down next to her.

Sven was murmuring to his screen, speaking of the records he wished to show. The first images revealed winged objects soaring over barren land and striking targets; others showed beams shooting out from globes that seemed to be orbiting Earth. A voice spoke of devices that could irradiate a city and kill its inhabitants, while leaving most of the buildings unmarked; another spoke of chemicals that poisoned land and water, and of microbes that could spread disease. Chemical symbols and images of microbes flickered on the screen. She had not imagined that there were so many ways to kill.

Images of large vehicles with treads were now moving across her screen, followed by helmeted figures carrying heavy rods. "That's how wars seemed to start," Sven said. "They'd use their smaller weapons first, ones that could kill only a few people or bring down a few aircraft. They'd destroy part of a city with bombs or try to get control of the other side's important places. They fought on the water, too, in ships that floated and ones that could go under the water." She saw winged vessels rise from what looked like a floating platform.

They had sent death into the air, over land, into Earth's oceans. She shuddered; they had surrounded themselves with death. "Didn't they see what they were doing?" she said faintly. "Why couldn't they stop?"

"They would, after a while, and then they'd fight some more. When they couldn't kill enough people with smaller weapons, they'd use more destructive ones. Sometimes they'd get scared of what they were doing, and sometimes they didn't seem to care after a while. It must have been like a game to some of them, the ones who weren't there to see people actually die. They'd just see diagrams on a screen, or people who might as well have been just images. Maybe that's how their violent time made them see others."

She closed her eyes, hating what she was.

"Have you seen enough?" Sven asked.

"Is that the worst of it?"

"No." His voice was strained. "I think the worst for me were the last images the mind received before it lost contact with the outside."

"Then I'll look at those, too."

He touched her arm lightly for a moment. "Nita—"

"Go on. Call them up."

He muttered to his screen. She saw what might have been a room, crowded with people; many were lying on the floor. Their faces were disfigured with sores or peeling skin; a few were only children. "These people are dying of a disease caused by a biological weapon," the mind's toneless voice said. "There is no one to help them, and no antidote for their disease."

The room disappeared; she was gazing at a group of people fleeing through a hallway. Walls buckled around them; she caught a glimpse of a woman trying to shield a child before a boulder crushed them. "A more primitive weapon is destroying that city," the mind said, "one that—"

She could take no more. She jumped to her feet and hurled the screen across the room. Her body was shaking; she was too stunned to cry. Hands gripped her wrists; she struggled, then leaned against the boy.

"I wish you hadn't seen it," he said.

"I had to know." She looked up at him and saw her despair reflected in his eyes. "It couldn't have ended that way. Some of them must have seen what was happening and stopped it. If the mind didn't see the rest, then maybe—"

"Then why haven't any of them come here? They're gone, Nita. Maybe we should be grateful for that." He released her and stepped back. "If our violent time comes, it'll be better if we're alone."

"I won't let it come. I won't let myself be like that." She sat down once more. Llipel and Llare must have seen these images and learned what they meant from the mind, yet they had allowed her and Sven to live. Did they hope or believe that she and the boy could avoid such brutal actions? Or were they simply waiting until that time came to act? Gentle though they were, they might be able to defend themselves if necessary; perhaps they were already prepared to do so. She could not know what other secrets they might be hiding.

"I've seen the worst," she said, trying to steady herself. "I'll try not to think about it too much. You can show me how to use the catalogue now."

"Nita—"

"Show me how."

After spending many days in the library, Nita had discovered that most of the records concerned the Institute's work. Only a few told her much about the world outside, and these were mostly of a practical nature—works about emergency medical procedures, the plants and animals in various regions of Earth, or the supplies one might need to carry when venturing into unpopulated regions. Apparently her people had sometimes sought separateness from their kind and the dwellings they had built; that knowledge brought a bitter smile. All of Earth was unpopulated now.

Some records went into more detail about the physiology of her people and the manner in which they had reproduced. Sven had no doubt looked at such records before. The subject was one they might have discussed, but she shrank from mentioning it to him, even though she had no cause to be embarrassed about the topic. Talking to him would be easy enough, but he might want to experiment, see if it was really the wonderful experience the screen images assured her it was, and she was not ready for that.

Even so, she often felt an odd lurching in her stomach when Sven's hand brushed against hers, or when she thought of what it might be like to press her lips to his, but she did not know where such actions might lead. Sometimes she felt warm as she thought of him, as though she were succumbing to one of the illnesses of her kind. She grew more conscious of the dark lashes around his blue eyes and the way his paler skin grew a little browner when he spent more time in the courtyard or garden.

But maybe he did not want to be any closer to her than he was already. She could understand that. What her people called love was one of their strong feelings, and could stir up other feelings she might not be able to control. Their love had not kept them from striking out at others; it seemed useless for anything except bringing young into the world. Llipel and Llare clearly had no need for love, and that might be why they seemed calm.

The few records of the life her people had led outside the Institute seemed to be stories of people rising to positions of power, ruling others, becoming honored, or being betrayed. Some were documents covering many hundreds of years, telling her of the rise and decline of various groups in different regions of Earth; these were listed in the catalogue under "History." Others, called "Literature," were different kinds of records, many telling only a story of a small group of people in a particular place during a short period of time, but most of them did little to give her a happier picture of her kind.

Her people seemed driven by passions and urges often outside their control. They made pledges and broke them, afflicted even those closest to them with lies and violence, loved and saw their love turn into indifference and hate, or become poisoned by what they called jealousy. They oppressed others of their kind and either took pleasure in that or convinced themselves it was necessary. They killed others in fits of rage, acts that were usually punished unless it was a time for war, when the same acts were praised.

Even when these stories ended happily, or the people in them relented and changed their ways, other stories told a similar painful tale all over again.

Throughout all the stories, she saw hints at other tales this library did not hold, though she might not have wanted to read or view them. The emptiness of the world outside told her that the last story of her people had ended badly.

She looked at the records of the Institute itself—its plans, its hopes, the meetings of the people who had worked there, and the students who had come to learn from them. She learned that fewer had come to the Institute over the years, that others had left, that finally only the cybernetic mind remained to watch over the place. The mind had once heard the voices of other minds far away, but those voices had fallen silent long ago. It had waited, but its creators had never spoken to it again.

Nita could imagine where the people here had gone— to fight their wars, to make certain that, in the end, no one was left to remember the Institute.

Sven splashed awkwardly to the side of the pool, then climbed up a ladder. Nita glanced at him, then looked away as he reached for his towel, reminding herself that she should not stare.

She poked at the towel wrapped around her wet hair, then pulled on her coverall. She had been teaching the boy how to swim, and he was now able to stay afloat, but his kicks and strokes remained clumsy. When they swam, or played games over the screens, or talked about some of the things their guardians had told them, they could be easier with each other. She could forget about what she knew for a while and could be grateful for a companion like herself.

The weather was warmer today. Sven tied his towel around his waist and sat down near their tray of food. She opened a container of soup, waited for it to warm up, then lifted it to her lips.

Sven was sipping his soup without slurping it today. Apparently he had also been getting instructions from the images about how to eat in another's company. It was a skill their guardians had never taught them.

"Would you care for a sandwich?" he said as he held out a package to her.

"No, thank you," she replied, wondering how their people had been able to function at all with all the rules they had carried in their heads.

"The warmer weather'll be here soon," Sven said. "The trees will be getting greener again."

She had never paid much attention to the changes of season. Colder weather meant racing for the east wing after leaving the warm water of the pool, while hot weather meant she could lie on the tiles until she was dry. She would have to pay more attention to the seasons if they were ever to explore the outside.

"Do you really think we'll ever know enough to go into the forest?" she asked.

"Why shouldn't we? The library has records. Our people were able to live in forests and other places in their earliest times. It's one of the few good things about them, that they were able to find ways to survive even when it must have seemed almost impossible."

"And look what it led to," she said.

"At least they weren't helpless. They didn't have to depend on a mind to take care of them. Llare and Llipel could have taken us outside. It's as if they wanted us to be helpless."

"I don't think so," she responded. "They're probably as afraid of the outside as we are." He was reminding her of her own suspicions.

Nita could not shake the feeling that her guardian was observing her more closely. Llipel was often staring at Nita when she awoke, as if she had been watching her all through the night. Occasionally, she had seen Llipel pacing near the entrance to the cold room, as if she was guarding it from Nita. Nita was authorized now; she could enter the place where she had been stored. But somehow she felt that Llipel might find a way to keep her from entering that room.

Sven had finished his food; he gazed past her, then picked up his coverall as he got to his feet. "I think I'll go to the courtyard. If you want, you can come over for our evening meal later." He paused and looked down at his feet. "I mean—well, I'd like it if you did."

"Then I will. I mean, I'd like to."

"Uh, excuse me."

He wandered off, obviously wanting to be alone at the moment. She sighed, wondering what he thought about when he wasn't with her, then stood up.

Llipel was standing by the entrance to the east wing. Nita felt a twinge of annoyance; how long had her guardian been watching them? She forced herself to smile as she walked toward Llipel.

Nita looked up from a text on microbiology and noticed that Sven had left the library. She had joined him there right after her morning meal; he had apparently crept from the room before she became aware of his absence.

Maybe he was tiring of her company. In recent days, he had seemed distracted during their talks or the meals they sometimes shared. He often wandered off to the walled-in courtyard, where he was usually exercising or running over the grass when she found him. She had seen him glance toward the wall, as if anxious to see what lay on the other side.

She lowered her eyes to the screen. There seemed to be more that she could not discuss with Sven lately. According to the records, those called women and those called men had led very different lives for much of their history. Often, the men had not even seen the women as people like themselves, and much of the violence the writings mentioned seemed to have been committed by men. Did that mean that men had more times of violence than did women? She could not be sure, but the records also showed that women were capable of abetting men in their violence, and in the end, both had brought about the war. Some stories had told her of women who had urged their mates and sons to fight; a time had come when women and men fought together. The women had become like the men; surely, if her people had possessed more control of their actions, it would have been the other way around.

Sven had to know this; he had read more records than she. But if she spoke to him about it, he might be hurt or angered and think she was comparing him to men of the past. He might even suppose that she was trying to escape her own shame over their kind's deeds by blaming them on his half of their species. She had seen enough of Sven by now to know that he was much like her, with the same questions, worries, and feelings. She did not want to believe that a difference that existed only so that their people could reproduce themselves could create more barriers between them.

The door slid open. She looked up, expecting to see Sven. Llare entered and sat down on the floor near the catalogue.

Nita lowered her reading screen to her lap. She had not yet spoken to Sven's guardian except in the boy's presence. "Greetings, Llare," she said.

"Sven is not with you." The fur on Llare's body was paler and less golden than Llipel's, but otherwise the two looked much the same. "There was a time when he came here more often. I had to remind him of his time for food or physical movement."

"The library's still newer to me than to him," Nita responded. "He's seen more records than I have."

"Perhaps that is the reason he is absent now, even

in this time of more togetherness for you." Llare combed the fur of one arm, then retracted his claws. "Have you learned much from this place?"

Nita nodded. "Yes, but—" She wasn't sure of what to say to Llare.

"What is it, Nita? Does this remain a time of more questions?"

"I think it's always a time of questions for us," she said. "It's just that so much is missing. Do you know what I mean? There were other places besides this Institute where people studied different things, but I haven't found much information about them here."

"Perhaps they had no need to keep such knowledge in this place."

"It isn't just that," Nita said. "I've read a lot about what our people did and thought, but I keep feeling that there's more about them that I don't see, that isn't here."

Llare gazed at her steadily. "And what does this bring you to think?"

"I don't know. They were driven to do such terrible deeds, but at least some of them seemed to think they could change. I can't see why they would have tried to accomplish so much if they knew it would be destroyed. And maybe they didn't all die in their last war. Maybe they were able to stop it before that happened."

"We saw none of your kind anywhere on this world."

"You and Llipel came here. Maybe they went to

another world." She was still trying to cling to that hope—that they might have changed and found another home elsewhere.

Llare waved one arm gracefully. "We saw no signs of that, no places that might have held such vessels. That does not mean that there were no ships, only that signs of them are not here. There is a crumbling that comes to things here—a decay. We know that your kind could launch vessels into space. You have seen images of such ships."

"Yes, I have," Nita replied. "Some of them were used to send weapons into orbit around Earth."

"And so perhaps they destroyed themselves completely, before they could leave this world. It is hard to know what to think. Most of their structures are gone, or are only ruins. Perhaps—"

"I keep telling myself that they would have left a message here if they were going off to fight, but the war could have come with no warning. If there had been survivors, they should have come here eventually. I tell myself that, and then I look at the mind's maps and see how far the Institute was from other places." She sighed. "I know what they were like, and yet I keep hoping some of them lived. That must seem strange to you."

"Much about your kind has always seemed strange." Llare gazed past Nita, eyes unreadable and blank, as Llipel's were when she was deep in thought. "I shall say my thoughts now. Llipel and I saw many records here. They seemed to say that a time of destruction came to your kind, one that they made for themselves. Then the time came for raising you and Sven, to devote ourselves to caring for you. I believed that watching you grow and seeing how you acted would answer some of our questions."

"And has it?"

"It has brought more questions. When Sven came to this room of records and learned of his kind, he felt what you call a despairing, but that made it easier for him to bear his life here. He did not long for other companions who might show the violence of your people." Llare paused. "But Sven could read records I could not, and learned more than I had seen. I saw from what he told me that much about your kind seemed unsaid or was missing. Now I wonder if we have a true picture of your people."

"Does Llipel wonder the same thing?"

"I do not know," Llare said. "We do not speak of such matters. We shared some observations of you and Sven, little more—it is not time for more. But Llipel has not gazed at the library's images for much time, or called them up on a screen. I would not have these new thoughts now if Sven had not shared what he learned with me."

"And what thoughts have you had?" Nita leaned forward, curious, but also afraid of what she might hear.

"There may be more to your people than this room of records shows. This room does not hold all knowledge about them, and we could not seek out other records in other places while we were caring for you. We thought your kind destroyed themselves. We believed that they must have been compelled to that, as Llipel and I seem compelled to stay apart. We feared the violence that might lie inside you and the boy when you met. But now that you are together with him, I wonder. Perhaps the wars of your people were not actions they had to follow."

"That's even worse," Nita said bitterly. "To think they couldn't help themselves is bad enough, but to think they chose—"

"This is a world where living things struggle and die and prey upon others, as the creatures in the forest outside still do. Your people were of this world. Your records say that long ages passed until their time of knowing themselves and their thoughts—even then, some of what they once were remained. They might have passed their time for fighting. They might be here, but hidden from us somehow. Perhaps they know Llipel and I are here, and will not show themselves until they know why. I cannot see how they could be hidden, but I do not know all about them. They might have a way."

Nita shivered, wondering if that could be true.

"And perhaps there is a purpose in the journey that brought me here," Llare continued. "Was there a struggle for us on our world? Is the space beyond this world a place of struggle? Perhaps destruction has come to other worlds. Perhaps this violence comes to all creatures. Llipel and I do not know our kind, what they are, or what our purpose might be. Another time is coming, Nita—I feel this without knowing why I do. Llipel and I will pass to another time, and I do not know what it will be—togetherness, perhaps, or—" Llare's claws scratched at the floor.

Nita was afraid to move. Llare suddenly stood up, in one fluid movement. "But this talk brings no answers. I leave you to your records now."

Nita stared after Llare until the door closed, then shrank back against the couch. Llare had said another time was coming. Perhaps the people of Earth weren't the only ones who sought the death of others; maybe Llare's people did as well. She could understand why Llare's kind might fear Earth's people; those who could kill so many of their own kind might be merciless toward others. Llare's people might want to make certain Earth could threaten no one else. Such a goal might have been hidden from Llipel and Llare until they learned more about Earth and any dangers they might face here—or else they knew and had kept their secret. Their gentleness might only be a deception.

Nita imagined other furred beings waiting in ships beyond Earth, waiting for the time when they could at last erase any remnant of Earth's people, when Llipel and Llare might come to see their purpose. Llare had spoken of a struggle. She thought of Llare's claws and seemed to feel them digging into her chest.

9

Dusky and Tanj were in the courtyard, prowling near the wall. Nita walked along one tree-lined path, calling out Sven's name, then saw that he was not there. She hurried back inside and went to the screen near the door.

"Where's Sven?" she asked.

"He is in the residential quarters on the fourteenth floor of the tower," the mind replied.

Turning away from the screen, she walked toward the corridor that led to the tower. She had been so preoccupied with the library's records that she had not yet bothered to explore much of the Institute.

As she strode between the walls of closed doors, she pondered what Llare had said. Nita's people couldn't be hidden here in the Institute or Llare and Llipel would have found them long ago. Neither did she imagine that they were lurking outside in the forest; vast as the woods were, there would have been some sign of their presence. But they might have found a way to conceal themselves elsewhere while Llipel and Llare were exploring this world.

She sighed. Perhaps she should not hope that her people would suddenly appear, or come to the Institute to fetch her and Sven. If they were as violent as the records showed they had been, and if they had reason to be suspicious of the alien visitors, they might not welcome two who had grown up with those who could be Earth's enemies.

Satisfying her curiosity had led her to this—revulsion at the acts of her kind and fear of Llipel and Llare.

She would have to tell Sven of her suspicions; she could not hide her thoughts from him. They might have to leave the Institute if what she suspected was true. But where could they go? How could they hide from the ship if Llipel and Llare pursued them? Where could they even begin to look for others of their kind? What would they do if more of Llipel's people came to Earth?

The door to the lobby slid open. She walked toward the lifts and entered one, so lost in her musings that she did not notice that the lift had stopped until a voice announced that she had reached the fourteenth floor.

A hallway stretched before her. A door opened; Sven wandered into the hall. She was surprised to see him in a pale brown shirt and loose dark brown trousers.

"Your clothes," she said.

He started, then came toward her; he was frowning. "If you knew I was here, couldn't you have told the screen you were coming?"

Stung, she stepped back. "I didn't think it mattered. If you wanted to be by yourself, you could have left a message on the screen saying so. I always do."

"It's all right." He lowered his eyes. "I'm just not— I'm still used to being by myself a lot of the time."

"I know," she said a little more gently. "I'm the same way sometimes."

"You can stay if you want. I mean, it's all right with me."

Sven was holding two objects in his hand that seemed like the foot coverings some of the screen images wore. "Where did you get those?" she asked. "And the clothes—where'd you find them?"

"In here." He pressed a door open; she followed him into a room. Two small couches and three chairs were grouped together near a window; he led her into an adjoining room, where a platform with two pillows stood against a wall.

He crossed the room and opened a wide panel in the opposite wall. "These clothes were here," he said. "I looked in some of the other rooms. Most of the closets were empty, or had clothes that wouldn't fit me." He dropped the two foot coverings. "I tried on these shoes, but they pinch my toes."

"I wonder why they left those things behind."

Sven's mouth twisted. "Anyone who could leave embryos behind in the cryonic facility probably wasn't paying attention to clothes. Maybe they didn't need them, or didn't have time to get them." He pulled a round, flat object from a shirt pocket. "I found this inside a jacket."

She peered at his find, which was marked with letters and held a small needle. "What is it?"

"A compass. The needle always points north, so you can tell where you're going. I read about compasses in the records. Somebody must have used it to go for walks in the woods. We might need it if we ever go exploring."

She was about to speak of her conversation with Llare, then caught sight of the small screen near the pillowed platform. She might give herself away if she said anything here; their guardians could be watching or might look at the mind's records later. She could ask the mind to close its sensors here, but she had not made such a request since becoming authorized. It might be better to speak to Sven where they could not be observed.

"Come on," Sven said as he left the room. She followed him into the hall and down to another numbered door. "I looked in this room before. There are some clothes here that might fit you. I was thinking of surprising you with them later." They entered another room with chairs and couches, then passed through a door into a room with a closet.

Nita opened the closet's panel. Three garments hung from a metal pole. She reached for a red shirt, marveling at the smoothness of the fabric, then removed a pair of black slacks. She had unzipped her coverall and was shrugging out of it before recalling that Sven was still in the room. Beate probably would have advised her to excuse herself first, but it was too late for that now.

He looked away, reddening a little, as she dressed. "It's a little loose," she said, plucking at the shirt, "and these pants are too long."

"Roll them up, then." He paused. "You look different."

"Different?"

"Better."

She smiled at the compliment, then stooped to roll up the trousers. "We could live in these rooms," he went on. "We'd have everything we need here. Llipel and Llare probably wouldn't mind."

Her pleasure at having the new clothes faded; he had reminded her of her fears. "It's something to think about," she said. "I'm glad you found the clothes. I was getting tired of coveralls."

"You look nicer than you did in coveralls."

"So do you," she responded. He smiled before she averted her eyes; all these compliments were making her feel awkward with him. "Sven, would you come to the lobby with me? There's something I want to do."

"Don't you want to look for more clothes?"

"Later, maybe. This is important."

He shrugged. "All right."

* * *

"What's so important?" Sven asked as they entered the lift.

"You'll see." They rode down to the lobby in silence; Sven seemed puzzled but did not speak.

"Well?" he said as they left the lift. "What is it?"

She walked toward the doors ahead without answering, not trusting herself to speak. As she approached the entrance, she slowed her steps, afraid that her fear might turn into panic. But she had been in the garden often enough; this couldn't be that different.

Sven said, "You want to go outside."

"Yes. You keep talking about exploring. We'll have to try it sooner or later."

He took a breath. "Might as well see what it's like." His voice shook a little.

They walked through one door as it opened, then down the steps that led to the ground. A flat, stony surface stretched before them, marred by a few cracks and strewn with bits of rubble. The sun was nearly overhead and the surface felt warm under her feet. A wind whipped past her, lashing her hair; it was stronger than any breeze she had ever felt in the garden. She shivered, aware that there were no walls here to protect them.

The desolation of the surface nearly overwhelmed her. "They came here," she said, "in their ships and hovercars. I used to think I'd see one someday." Her voice sounded weak and small.

"I've seen the images. I wish we had one of those hovercars—we could have done a lot of exploring in one." He glanced at her. "We really are alone. Don't you feel it? It's hard to imagine anyone coming here now."

She moved farther away from the steps. She was struggling against the urge to flee back to the lobby, to safety, then reminded herself that the Institute might not be safe for long. The surface under her feet was fairly smooth, but avoiding the rubble slowed her steps. Sven trailed after her, treading carefully on the expanse.

"Is this what you wanted to see?" he asked. "Expecting visitors?" He made a small, choked sound that might have been a laugh as he came to her side. They gazed at the edge of the wood to the south. She wondered how she could ever bring herself to enter the forest and to face whatever dangers lay there.

I'm wrong about our guardians, she thought; I have to be wrong.

She glanced back at the tower, then continued to walk until they reached the eastern edge of the surface. In the distance, a mower was clipping the grass bordering the east wing; the robot was too far away for the mind to hear them through its sensors.

Sven's lips were pressed tightly together. He was clearly as anxious as she was to go back inside, although he probably would not admit it.

She said, "I have to talk to you. That's the real

reason I wanted to come out here. It may be important, and I didn't want to say anything to you inside."

"What is it?"

"Llare talked to me today, in the library." She told him quickly about what his guardian had said, and then mentioned her own suspicions. Sven was silent as she spoke. A grim look had come into his eyes by the time she was finished.

He thrust his hands into his pockets and paced over the grass as she waited for his reaction. Perhaps he would convince her that she was mistaken.

He stopped pacing. "I wish I could say you're probably wrong," he said at last, "but I've been wondering some of the same things lately. I keep asking myself how they could have come here without knowing anything about their kind—their people couldn't have sent them here for no reason. And if they're here because of an accident, or because they were lost somehow, there'd be no reason to hide that. I told myself I was imagining things, but now I don't know. If you have the same ideas—" He sighed. "And now you say that Llare told you another time's coming. That doesn't sound good."

"What'll we do?"

"What can we do?" His eyes narrowed. "They kept us here. We don't know how to survive outside. They didn't tell us about each other—I think I started doubting Llare the first time I saw you. If they could deceive us about that, they could lie about their real reasons for being here. Maybe some of our people are alive, and they're keeping that from us, too. After all, they didn't tell us about each other."

She tensed. "Do you think—"

"I don't know. You say Llare talked of a struggle. Maybe they're here to make sure all of our people are dead."

"But why would they bring us up?" she asked. "Why didn't they let us die? Why did they repair the Institute's power source instead of letting the place rot? For that matter, why didn't they destroy all the embryos in the cold room after they knew what was there?"

"How can we know?" he responded. "Maybe they wanted to study us first. And how can we be sure they didn't destroy everything in the cold room? We've never been inside, and separate circuits control it. Maybe there's nothing left—maybe they took care of that after they took us out. Llare told me never to go there, because he was afraid I might make his mistake, and we couldn't get in without authorization, anyway, but maybe he just wanted to see that I didn't find out what they'd done. Even the mind isn't linked to those circuits."

Nita sank to the ground, stunned by the horror of that possibility. She had been hoping for reassurance from Sven; instead, he had magnified her fears. She was beginning to see that the boy was ready to accept the darkest possibilities, while she still fought against believing the worst.

"They couldn't," she said. "They—" She gazed at

him as he sat down in front of her. "We're authorized now. We could go to the cold place anytime. They know that, and they can't really prevent it, can they?"

"They haven't had to try, really. They knew we wouldn't want to go there, even now. I could find out about my parents now, but I'm afraid to. I guess I just don't want to hear that the two people who created me went off to kill other people and die, and that's what I'd find out. In a way, it's easier if I don't hear it."

That was true, she thought. The cryonic facility still frightened her; the prohibition Llipel had placed on her was still strong. She was afraid to confront the room where potential members of her kind were suspended between life and nonexistence; she shrank from learning of the two parents who had left her there. She did not want to stand in a place that would remind her that only chance and a mistake had enabled her to live at all.

"How can we stay here, Sven?" she asked. "Where can we go?"

"We can't leave yet, not until we know more about how to survive." He drew his brows together. "Trouble is, we don't know what they might be able to do. They learned a lot here—they may have ways to protect themselves we don't know about. They might have weapons on their ship."

"Maybe we're wrong," she said desperately, wanting to wish away her suspicions. "Maybe we *are* just imagining things. We don't want to believe that our people were the only ones who could do evil things, and now we're coming up with reasons to see our guardians as enemies."

He gripped her arm. "Listen, whether we're right or wrong about this, the only safe thing to do is to protect ourselves somehow. If we're right, we have to figure out a way to escape them, and if we're wrong, it won't matter." He let go of her and rested his chin against his knee. "Let's assume that they kept some secrets just to protect us, and that they're honest about not knowing why they're here. Maybe they are as kind as they seem. They might not hurt us, but that doesn't mean others of their kind couldn't. They might just be waiting until it's time."

"I've been feeling that Llipel's watching me more," she admitted. "I never really feared that before—it only annoyed me once in a while." She bowed her head. "I don't want to believe any of this, and then I think of what Llare said."

"At least we're together in this, Nita. They don't know what we think yet. As long as they don't, we've got some time." He was silent for a moment. "I wish we had weapons of some kind, just in case. If they have a time for fighting, too, they may not be able to control their actions."

She grimaced, sick at the thought. "Well, there aren't any weapons here."

"How do we know? We never asked the mind. Somehow, considering what I know about our people, I can't believe they wouldn't have had weapons of some sort here." He stood up, then helped her to her feet. "We'd better go and find out."

The desks inside the lobby's transparent booth held small screens that lay flat against the desktops. Sven lifted one screen until it locked into place.

"If we're going to explore the forest," he said, "we may need some way to protect ourselves against dangerous animals. Are there any weapons here?"

"You are not authorized to have that information," the mind replied. "I cannot answer."

"But I have authorization," Sven protested.

"I see no security guard's medallion."

Sven tapped his fingers on the desktop, then began to search through the desk drawers. He pawed through a pile of authorizations, then lifted a chain from which a circular disk dangled. "Is this a medallion?"

"It is," the voice replied. Sven hung the chain around his neck. "You may now enter the door marked SE-CURITY in the hallway that leads from the lobby into the garden. You will be issued your weapon there."

Sven rummaged in the drawer, then handed Nita another disk. "That was easy enough."

Too easy, she thought; Llipel and Llare had to know about these weapons. Could that mean they had intended no harm? Or had they only supposed that their claws might be defense enough against a helpless, unarmed child?

They went to the hallway. The door marked SE-CURITY opened; on the opposite wall, slim metal rods with curved grips were held to the wall by clamps. Sven strode toward the wall and reached for a rod; the clamp snapped open as he gripped the wand in his hand. "Go ahead, Nita."

She forced herself to take one. A button was on the spot where the grip met the silvery rod; she was afraid to touch it. She looked toward the screen near the door. "Tell us how to use this," she said.

The tiny figure of a man appeared on the screen. "You must hold it in this way, aim at your target, and press the button firmly with your forefinger." The man turned and aimed; a beam shot out from the rod. "The beam will stun the target and cause a loss of consciousness for a period of five to ten minutes, thus allowing you time to apply restraints."

She let out her breath, relieved that the weapons were apparently not lethal. "We'll have to practice," Sven said. "Hitting a target probably isn't so easy."

"After you have fired approximately forty times," the screen continued, "return it to its holder. It will recharge within an hour. A reminder—be certain to keep your weapon in its belt when it is not in use. It will not fire unless it is taken from the belt and pressure is applied by your finger."

"Where are the belts?" Sven asked.

"Open the panel to your right."

Sven went to that side of the room; the panel slid open. He took out two belts and handed one to Nita, then slipped the other around his waist before sliding

106

the wand into the belt's leather sheath. "Strange," he muttered. "They had weapons that could destroy the world, and these only stun."

She put on her own belt. The weapon seemed light; she could almost forget it was there.

She turned and left the room, hating the thought of any weapon at all. She was halfway across the lobby before Sven caught up with her. "I know how you feel," he said, "but we *will* need them if we go exploring."

She moved toward the doors; he followed her outside. She descended the steps and sat down on the bottom one as he seated himself next to her. "I'll tell that to myself," she said, "that I may need it only in the forest and not in here."

"Nita, I talked about staying in the tower before. Maybe that's what we should do. We can tell Llipel and Llare that we want to be by ourselves. They probably won't object, and it might be safer for us."

She wondered if she could hide in the tower tormented by her doubts. "We'll have to ask them."

"I'll talk to Llare over the screen."

"I think I'd rather go to Llipel and tell her myself. She might find it odd if I just ask her over the screen. Anyway, there's something else I should do."

"What?"

She turned toward him. "I think I should see the cold room now."

He shook his head vehemently. "But you don't know—"

107

"Then I'd better find out. It makes more sense than sitting here dwelling on horrible things that might not even be true."

"But it might not prove anything even if they've left it alone," he said. "Maybe they just haven't had to act yet."

"At least I could put it out of my mind for now."

"If you're going to go there," he said, "I should come with you."

"No, Sven. You can watch me through the screen, at least when I'm outside the cold place. I think I can take care of myself, but if anything happens, you'll be safe and can decide what to do then." She tried to smile. "Do you think I'd do this if I really believed the worst? I have to prove you're wrong about that, even if you might be right about other things."

"Believing the worst," he said, "may be the only thing that can protect us now."

"All the more reason for you to stay in the tower."

He glanced at her. "I still think you shouldn't go alone, but I can't force you to bring me along, and you have that weapon now. I hope you can use it if you have to."

"It won't come to that. If Llipel says she doesn't want me to go to the cold room, I'll come back here. She'll never know why I wanted to see it."

"And then what?"

"Then we can assume the worst, I suppose." She stood up and began to climb the steps.

108

10

Nita walked slowly through the garden, her body taut with tension. Llipel had no reason to harm her yet and could not suspect her doubts. She would be safer if she acted as though she had nothing to fear from her guardian.

She hesitated in front of the entrance, then opened the door. The screen inside told her that Llipel was in the cafeteria.

She went there and found Llipel on the floor, chewing at a flat, bluish cake she held in her hands. A few other provisions from the ship were piled on the table nearest her. She lifted her head and gazed calmly at Nita.

"Sven and I were in the tower," Nita said. "That's where I found these clothes." She pulled at the sleeve of her red shirt. "We went outside, too, just for a little while—we didn't go far. We're thinking of staying in the tower for a bit, just for a change and to be by ourselves. We might—well, we're thinking of exploring the forest after we've learned more about the outside." Her voice caught in her throat. She was babbling, trying to explain too much.

Llipel finished her food. Her black eyes widened a little, as if she was concerned. Now that Nita was in her guardian's presence, her suspicions seemed unfounded. This was Llipel, who had tended her when she was unable to care for herself, who had always reacted to her with gentleness.

"Will you want the cats in the tower as well?" Llipel asked.

"Oh." Nita had forgotten the cats. "I don't know. We'd have to take them down in the lift every time they want to go into the garden. But it would be nice to have them around."

"You might leave them in the garden and bring them to the big tower room when you like."

Dusky had never gone to Llipel as readily as to her. Nita had thought little of that before; living with a cat had shown her how independent and unpredictable such creatures could be, and Sven had told her that Tanj was even more temperamental. Now she wondered if the cats had somehow sensed a threat from Llipel and Llare.

"They were in the courtyard earlier," Nita said. "I'll have to get them later."

110

"There is no need. I shall ask Llare to let them into the garden for you."

Nita was still standing near the door. She forced herself to move closer to Llipel, afraid as she was of being too near her. "Have you eaten?" Llipel continued. "It is past the time of your midday eating."

Nita wanted to bolt from the room. "I'm not hungry. I can eat later." She sat down as Llipel brushed a few crumbs from her fur; she had never noticed how sharp her guardian's teeth and claws were before. Since meeting Sven, she had become more aware of the differences between her and Llipel, differences that now seemed ominous and menacing. Would she have been so ready to see them if she hadn't met the boy? Did being with one like herself have to separate her from others?

Llipel had said nothing about the weapon hanging from Nita's belt. Nita gestured at the wand. "Sven says we'll need a way of protecting ourselves when we go outside, so we asked the mind if it had anything."

"Will you go outside so soon?"

"Oh no. We'll have to practice before we do, and get used to being outside first. We didn't want to stay out long, it's—" Nita waved a hand. "We're accustomed to the garden and the courtyard. It's different when there aren't any walls to protect you."

"Then it will soon be time for you to see some of your world."

Nita averted her eyes. Llipel did not seem puzzled by or suspicious of her behavior; she did not even seem worried by the weapon. "I really wish we didn't have to have these wands," she murmured, "but we should be prepared when we go outside."

"Of course. We knew about the room of wands. I would have told you of it if we had gone outside together, but it may be better if you learn of this world with Sven. Be careful—it would be a loss if harm came to you. I want you safe, but it seems it is a time for you to reach out."

Her words did not ease Nita. The concern might be false, the kindly words a lie. She could read no hidden meaning in any gesture of Llipel's; her furred body was still, her hands resting on the floor.

"There's something I want to do before I go back to the tower," Nita said. "I've wanted to for a while, but I think this is the time."

"And what is that?" Llipel asked.

Nita took a breath. "I want to see the cold room. I want to go there." She watched her guardian, expecting to see signs of distress. "I'm authorized now, so I don't really have to ask you, but I hope you won't tell me not to go. I want to see where I was, where I came from."

Llipel thrust out an arm, as if pushing something away from herself, a sign of denial. "You should not."

Nita's muscles were stiff. She tried to keep her hand near her weapon without being obvious about it. "Why? I'll be careful, I won't make your mistake."

"I do not fear a mistake," Llipel replied. "I fear what you might feel when you stand near all that remains

112

of your people. Your feelings may move you to ask for another to live. We cannot know what that might bring."

"I won't do that," Nita said.

"Yet a time may come for such an action. I have thought much about what I once supposed about your kind. I feel that another time is approaching. A new feeling grows inside me that I cannot stop, as if a part of me is awakening."

Nita was terrified. Somehow, she managed to stand up; she felt as though her legs would give way at any moment. "I want to see the cold room." She waited, expecting Llipel to make another gesture of denial.

"Then you must go," Llipel said, surprising her. "But I cannot let you go there alone." She rose to her feet as Nita backed toward the door.

As they strode through the hall, Nita remained behind Llipel, keeping her guardian in sight. Why had Llipel agreed to this? It had to mean there was nothing to hide, that Sven's wild suppositions weren't true.

They came to the end of the corridor. Ahead lay the exit that led to Llipel's ship; to the left stood the door marked AUTHORIZED PERSONNEL ONLY with its diagram of a fetus. Llipel turned toward the door and said, "We wish to enter. We want only to view the place inside and what it holds." She glanced at Nita. "Be careful in what you speak."

The door opened slowly. Nita followed Llipel inside, too numb with fright to turn back. Her fear of her guardian had subsided a little; now it was the cold room she feared more.

They were in a small room. Behind glassy doors, a row of silvery suits dangled from hooks. Globes that might have been a kind of head covering sat above them on a shelf, while a row of boots stood on the floor. "Put on the protective clothing," a voice said. "Make sure that your helmet is securely sealed by your suit collar."

"I came here many times before I understood those words," Llipel murmured, "before I had enough of your speech to grasp them. The space inside must be kept free of what is on our bodies—the tiny things."

"Microbes," Nita said. Llipel opened the glass panel, pulled out a garment, and got into it quickly. The suit was too loose around her slender torso, while its five-fingered gloves were too large for her six-fingered hands. She held out a smaller suit.

Nita stared at the silvery garment, wondering what to do with her wand and belt. "Leave your wand here," Llipel said. "This is not a place for it."

She had no choice. She unhooked her belt, laid the weapon on the floor, and pulled the suit on over her clothes. She bent over to put on a pair of boots, then secured a helmet over her head.

Llipel covered her head with another helmet. The inner door opened. They entered a large room; its walls seemed to stretch the length of this wing. The wall to her left was filled with slots, each with a row of lights beneath it. From the bottom of each slot, slender tubes

114

nearly as thin as wires were connected to curved metallic chambers resting on a platform that ran the length of that wall. Each slot, she knew from diagrams she had seen, held an embryo; a tube would convey it to one of the chambers below.

The wall to her right was covered with shelves holding glassy boxes of various sizes, each covered with wires and tubes. Through the pale mist inside them, she glimpsed a few creatures that might have been cats, as well as the shapes of other animals she had viewed on the screens—dogs, monkeys, and small birds.

Llipel gestured to the right. "I found the cat for you there," her voice said inside Nita's helmet. "And you were over here." She motioned to the left. "Llare found the boy at the other end of the room, where it meets the west wing."

The lights under the slots had already told Nita what she wanted to know. She thought of the diagrams the library's records had shown. Had there been no embryos in the slots, the lights would have gone out. But the library and its records had not prepared her for this sight.

Hundreds of her kind, maybe more, had to be housed here, dependent on the circuits that protected them. She swayed unsteadily. "They're safe."

"Yes," Llipel said, "safer than they would be inside the bodies of your kind."

"Of course they are safe," another voice said inside Nita's helmet. "They are stored and ready to be revived. Do you wish to revive one? Say the names of its parents, and it will be conveyed from its container to a womb, to begin gestation. Which do you wish to revive?" The voice paused. "If necessary, I can recite the names of parents, and the requisite facts about each, if you are selecting one for adoption."

"No," Nita said quickly. "We don't want to revive anyone." She moved toward the wall, then felt a tug on her arm. Llipel's gloved hand was holding her; she nearly recoiled.

"You were there," Llipel said. Nita saw then that the lights under one slot did not shine.

She shuddered, as if feeling the cold through her suit. "My parents," she said. "I think I can ask it now. I might as well know. Who were they?" She shook off Llipel's grip, then touched the surface of the slot that had once held her. "I was here, and Llipel revived me. Tell me who my parents were."

"Your mother was called Juanita Gutiérrez," the voice replied. "Your father's name was Robert Kufakunesu. If you would like to know—"

"Why did they come here?"

"For the reasons many came—they had hopes for a child but were not yet ready to raise one. At the time they arrived, the Institute was just beginning its work. They were willing to take this chance of having a child they could remove and raise later, when one or both of them might no longer be able to have a child in any other way. They were to contact the Institute when it was time to begin gestation, then return for their child at the time of its birth."

116

"Why didn't they return, though?" she said. "Was it a war? Did they die before they could come back?"

"Do not ask this," she heard Llipel say.

"I know nothing about any war preventing their return," the voice said. "My records show that the Institute sent them messages when they were living in your father's African land. It seems that they had second thoughts and chose not to raise a child. There were others who never returned. Occasionally, those they left here were later adopted by others, but many were not. The Institute expanded enough as the years passed to store more embryos. There was hope all might be claimed in time, and by then some people saw reasons for keeping these specimens of humanity preserved, and envisioned a time when they might be needed."

"Because of the last war," Nita whispered. "Because there might not be anyone else left."

"It seems so. There was much talk of a war during the last days people were here, but even before then, many had left this place. Perhaps people no longer needed this Institute. Fewer came, more rooms were closed and left empty, and resources were directed elsewhere, perhaps to their weapons. The Institute's administrators could find few willing to accept the potential children stored here. Many of the parents were like yours and decided against coming here for their children. In the end, there was only silence for me, until the two called Llare and Llipel came to this place. That is all I can tell you, unless you would like to know

117

more about your parents. I can call up records of them."

"No," she said softly. Her parents had forgotten her; the world had found no place for her. By the time of the last war, she had already been cast away by the two who should have cared most for her. None of her people had wanted her. Only a cybernetic intelligence, following ancient commands, had preserved her. She was alive only because of Llipel, who might finally turn from her, too.

Llipel's arms were suddenly around her. "I did not want you to hear such words," her guardian said. "I know what it is to seem cast away by one's kind. I am sorry, Nita. I would close off this time for you and carry you to another, but I cannot. I thought you would be told that the two called parents had died before you were claimed, but this is as painful to hear."

Nita twisted away. Llipel began to paw at her helmet with her gloved hands in her sign of distress.

"You should have let them die," Nita cried. "I'm glad their parents are dead. No one cared about them then, there's no one left to care about them now. I don't know why you bothered to raise me." She panted for breath. "There's no reason to bother with them now. They can just wait here until the mind begins to fail, or the circuits aren't replaced, or until everything in this place has vanished or rotted away. They're already forgotten—they might as well be dead."

"Nita—"

She ran from the room, pausing only long enough to pick up her weapon before she rushed into the hall.

118

As she tore the helmet from her head and was about to hurl it away, she remembered that Sven was probably watching her.

She moved toward the nearest screen and tried to compose herself. "Sven, everything's all right. You don't have to worry. I'll come there later." She turned away from the screen before she could see his image, stumbled toward the exit, and went outside.

11

Nita circled Llipel's ship. She had never been this close to it before, but had only watched from the doorway whenever her guardian went out to the vessel. The door had always closed behind Llipel so that Nita could not follow.

The silver globe was not that large; she doubted that the inside could be much bigger than the room in which she and Llipel slept. How far could the two have traveled in such a small ship? She had learned enough from the Institute's records about the solar system to know that her guardian's people had to be from somewhere much farther away. The planets around Earth's sun were not places where they could have survived easily, if at all. Perhaps they had a base on one of the satellites of Mars, or on Earth's moon. Maybe Llare and Llipel had a way of communicating with such a base, and had kept that a secret, too.

She stopped next to one of the globe's three legs. A ladder led up to the ship, but she could see no opening. For a moment, she was tempted to climb the ladder, but doubted that the ship would open to her. Llipel and Llare were not likely to leave the vessel unprotected now that Nita and Sven could go outside.

She turned away from the ship and walked across the grass, keeping near the Institute as she glanced toward the forest. The more she learned, the crueler her world became. She could almost understand why her people had sought death; maybe the pain and neglect they had inflicted on one another were finally too much for them to bear.

Rubble crunched under her boots; she had reached the expanse in front of the Institute. She strode across the flat surface and sat down on the steps leading into the tower.

"Nita."

She looked up; Sven was coming down the steps. "You said nothing was wrong," he continued, "but you didn't look as though that was true. I was worried."

"Nothing happened to the cold room. They're all there and safe enough, if that makes any difference."

"You don't look very relieved."

"I found out a few things," she said. "I heard about my parents."

"You'd better come inside. We can talk there now. I spoke to Llare after you came out of the cryonic facility. I told him it was our time for togetherness now and that we didn't want to be observed. He asked me if it was our time for what our kind calls love, and I let him believe that—he knows our people liked to be alone then."

She was silent.

"Please come inside," he said. "Llare's asked the mind to close its sensors in the tower so we can have privacy. It won't open them again without our authorization. You don't have to worry."

She stood up and let him lead her inside. He guided her toward one side of the lobby; they sat down on the long, cushioned platform. "What happened, Nita?"

"I found out why my parents never came here for me. It wasn't because of the war. Apparently they came here long before that. They decided they didn't want me, they changed their minds, and no one else ever wanted me, either."

Sven cleared his throat. "Maybe that's not so bad. Isn't it better than finding out that the war killed them, or that they died fighting in it?"

"I don't know what to think!" she cried. "I don't know how I'm supposed to feel about anything, I don't even know what I am! I can't be like Llipel, and I don't want to be like our kind! Is that what I'll turn into—someone who can't care about anything, who acts like them?"

"I know, Nita. I'm not sure of what I am, either." He paused. "I don't think I want to know about my own parents. Look at it this way—we're alive because they didn't come for us."

She stood up, took off her boots, then removed the protective suit, folding it up before putting it on the floor. "I suppose that's better than dying the way our people did," she said.

"And maybe our parents didn't think of us as real. In a way, we weren't yet—they wouldn't even have been able to see us without looking through a microscope. They didn't really know us."

"But if they took the trouble to come here, shouldn't they have cared about what happened to us later?" She rubbed at her eyes. "Llipel was trying to console me when I heard the truth. I was so afraid of her, and now—" She looked down at the weapon and belt that lay next to her silver suit. "I feel horrible about distrusting her."

"I know," Sven said. "Llare still seems so kind and understanding. I wish we could trust them, but until we're sure, we should be careful."

He stood up and walked toward the booth. She followed him inside and watched as he rummaged in the desk drawers, searching every one until a pile of chains and medallions was heaped on one desk.

"That's all of them," he murmured. "We'll find a place to hide them up in the residential quarters. They won't be able to get at the weapons."

"They may have weapons of their own."

"At least they won't get ours."

* * *

They shared their evening meal in the large cafeteria on the fifteenth floor. There were foods here Nita had never seen in the east wing—chunks of a fishy substance in a light sauce, tiny vegetables prepared in unfamiliar ways, small cakes, and a pinkish liquid that made her feel light-headed after only one glass.

Tempting as the food was, Sven seemed to be eating very little. He had been more cheerful when they were practicing with their wands in the garden and had talked of how they might begin to explore the forest. Then he had aimed at a bird in one of the trees, expecting only to stun it, but the bird had been dead when he picked it up.

They had learned that their wands could kill smaller creatures, and that was probably useful to know, so that they would not be reckless. She was grateful that they hadn't aimed at the cats. But the incident had dismayed him.

Sven was picking at his food with his fingers. He had already given up trying to eat with the metal implements their kind had used to dine on certain foods. He had nodded at her attempts at conversation, but said little himself.

She was beginning to notice small differences in their reactions. However unhappy she got, her sorrowful moods passed before too long; Sven's moods seemed to have a deeper hold on him. She wondered what this meant. How different had individuals of their kind been from one another? Releasing one's anger could hurt someone else; holding it in might only make it worse for oneself. There seemed no purpose in having such feelings.

She suddenly yawned. Sven looked up. "You're tired."

"I guess I am." She set down her knife and fork. "Maybe I should go to sleep."

"The mind'll let us know if anyone enters the tower," he said, "but I don't think anyone will. They know we want to be alone. The cats should be all right in the garden."

"Are you going to sleep, too?"

He poured more of the pink liquid into his glass. "I think I'll stay up for a while."

"Do you want me to stay with you, then?"

"You don't have to. I'm used to being alone."

"Good night, Sven." He turned away as she got up and walked toward the lift.

She had left the silver suit in one of the rooms on the fourteenth floor, next to the room Sven had decided to use. Her closet held no clothing, but a door near it led to a small lavatory, where she discovered a stall in which she could bathe under a stream of water.

She left the lavatory, deciding she would wash in the morning, and settled on the room's pillowed platform. Tired as she was, she wondered if she would be able to sleep. Was it only that morning when Llare had spoken to her? Was it only thirty days ago that she had believed herself to be alone in the Institute with her guardian and Llare? It seemed much longer ago, part of a time when, whatever her sorrows, she had felt protected and safe.

Sven claimed that they had to act as though their fears were fact. She wasn't sure she believed that. How would they ever regain the goodwill of Llipel and Llare if the two realized they had been doubted and feared? Distrust and suspicion might widen the breach; trust would be difficult to regain. She and Sven might only bring about what they most feared and lead their guardians to conclude that Earth's people were indeed dangerous.

She was about to unbutton her shirt and prepare for sleep when she leaned toward the small screen near the platform. "I'd like to speak to Llipel," she said quickly, before she could have second thoughts.

Her guardian's golden-furred face suddenly appeared. "I have been concerned for you," Llipel said. "I was sorry I could not ease you."

"I know."

"You are with the boy now. Llare tells me that you wish to be by yourselves during your time of togetherness. Perhaps that will ease you."

"I'm all right now," Nita said. "I wanted you to know."

Llipel was silent for a bit, then said, "I will tell you this. Another time is coming, not just for you and the boy, but for us. Another change is near, and I do not know what it will bring, but no harm will come to you. You have nothing to fear from me—of that I am certain, though I do not know how I know this."

126

Nita tensed. She and Sven hadn't fooled Llipel at all. She lowered her eyes, tormented by her inability to trust her guardian even now. "It may be," Llipel went on, "that a time of silence will come when I no longer speak to you, but I will not forget you. I feel— but I cannot put it into your words."

Llipel sounded almost as if she was trying to say farewell. Nita was about to speak when the door opened; Sven entered the room.

"Thank you for telling me this," Nita said. "Good night, Llipel."

"Good night." The image vanished.

Sven stepped toward the platform; he seemed a little unsteady on his feet. "What was that all about?"

"I had to speak to her," she answered. "I didn't want her worrying about me after the way I acted in the cold room. She sounded strange, Sven. She says another time's coming, that she may not speak to me after a while, but that I have nothing to fear."

"Somehow that doesn't sound comforting."

She leaned back against the pillows. "Did you ever think that maybe they're testing us, trying to find out what we'll do now? We're so quick to see them as threats, even after all the years they've looked after us. Our kind seemed to see everything as a threat or an enemy."

"Not everything. We can trust each other, can't we?" He sat down on the platform next to her.

He seemed to want companionship now; he reached for her hand. She let him hold it, surprised at how moved she was by the gesture. "It wasn't a lie, what I told Llare," he said, "that I wanted to be alone with you for a while."

Her cheeks grew warm as she smiled. "I feel the same way," she said softly. His arms were around her; she leaned against him, welcoming his touch. She thought of how she had snuggled up to Llipel and had been comforted by her warmth. She had missed such closeness.

Sven stroked her arm gently. She pressed closer to him; his cheek brushed against hers. Her arms were around his waist; she trembled a little, surprised at the pleasure she felt.

His hand pulled at her shirt. A wilder feeling welled up inside her, and then she was afraid. "Nita," he whispered. "I want to—I can't stop thinking about it."

She drew back a little. "No, Sven. We can't—"

"It's all right." He held her more tightly. "I have an implant. I got one a little while after I first talked to you. I knew what could happen, and so did Llare. I asked him to help implant it, and he did."

"I can't."

"Nothing will happen. Isn't this what we're supposed to do?" He pressed his lips against her neck; she tried to push him away, but his grip was too strong. "I want this so much—it has to be time."

She twisted away. "No!" He reached for her; she jumped to her feet. "I'm not ready for this!"

"Then why did you let me hold you before?"

She could not answer.

128

"What do you want, then?" His face was drawn, his eyes angrier than she had ever seen them. "You didn't seem to mind at first."

"It isn't supposed to be like this."

"How do you know?" he said. "I just want to do what our people did when they were together. I can't put it out of my mind. What do you want? All those words I've seen in some of the stories about how I love you and I can't live without you? Well, I can't, can I? You're the only one of my kind here. Who else can I go to?"

"I don't want this."

"You could try. I can't believe you don't feel it, too." He started toward her and grabbed at her arm. She pulled free and yanked her weapon from its sheath.

"Don't come near me!" she shouted, shocked at her own rage. "You aren't thinking of me, just of what you want. I've read the records, I know what some men did to women, forcing themselves on them and hurting them and not caring about their feelings. Is that what you're like?"

His face paled. "That's what you think? I wouldn't have hurt you. Do you think you're any better? Look at you—you're ready to fight the only one of your kind left."

Her arm fell. He spun around and strode from the room. She let the wand drop to the floor, then threw herself across the platform.

She had wanted him closer to her, at least in the beginning. Why hadn't he seen that his embrace might have been enough? Had she made some sort of mistake and led him to think she wanted more? She had felt almost as if an enemy was with her, one who saw her only as something to be overcome.

She buried her head in a pillow, holding back her tears.

She was awake. Nita rubbed her eyes and sat up. A glance toward the window revealed a bright, sunlit sky; she had overslept.

She went into the lavatory and splashed cold water on her face as she thought of Sven. Another floor of residential quarters lay beneath this one; she could always live there. She was used to being alone; Sven would understand. Maybe he would want to keep away from her now.

She left the lavatory and saw that her weapon was still on the floor. She picked it up, then thrust it into her belt.

I don't want to fight, she thought. They would have to reach some sort of agreement. She was the only one Sven could turn to; he had said so the night before. If others had lived, he could have gone to someone else.

That notion was a knife stabbing inside her, bringing pain, anger, and a feeling of helplessness and desperation. She realized that she was feeling what some of the records called jealousy, that she could feel it even when no one lived who could take the boy from her. The feeling was poisonous; she could rid herself of it only by reaching out to him.

* * *

130

Sven was sitting at a table near the lift as she entered the cafeteria. He lifted his head; dark circles were under his eyes.

She walked toward him. "Are you still angry?" he asked.

"No."

"I don't know what happened to me. I had these feelings, but I could ignore them before. Then I was holding you and I couldn't think of anything else, and when you tried to pull away, I didn't know what to do."

"I had some feelings, too, at first, and then I was frightened."

"Even when you knew about my implant and that nothing could happen?"

She nodded. "I was confused. All these feelings came at once—wanting to be close, feeling happy, and being afraid."

"Then you said I was like those men who forced themselves on women. It was like saying I was worse than you, or was something else you weren't. But maybe I *am* like that. Maybe that's what I'll become."

"No." She sat down across from him. "I won't believe it. I wouldn't have said it if I hadn't read some of those stories. You're not like that, I know you're not. We don't have to be the way they were."

"You sound as though we have a choice."

"It's better to think that we do," she replied.

"And we can still be friends?"

"Of course."

He stood up and paced toward the windows. She was about to speak when he motioned to her. "Nita, come here. There's something below you should see."

She hurried toward him, then peered down through a pane at the garden. Llipel and Llare were sitting together under a tree; Llipel leaned toward her companion and gestured with her hands.

Sven let out his breath. "I think their time for separateness is over."

12

"It seems," Llipel said, "that you can protect yourself when you go into the forest."

Nita lowered her weapon. She had been preparing to fire at a rock Sven was about to hurl into the air. "I'm better at it," she said, "but it'll be harder to hit a target out there."

"You will have to keep close to this place when you first explore, until you grow used to the forest," Llipel replied.

Llare descended the ship's ladder; the opening above him had disappeared. Sven turned as his guardian went to Llipel's side. For days, Nita had rarely seen the two apart. They often went to their ship when Sven and Nita were outside practicing with their wands; at other times, their guardians sat together and watched them in silence. It was strange to see them together so much, and even more unnerving to sense their eyes on her as she aimed and fired. They seemed unperturbed by the weapons, but they could be looking for weaknesses, trying to see how well she and the boy could defend themselves.

"You're improving," Sven muttered.

"That isn't saying much," Nita responded. She usually hit her target only when it wasn't moving.

"Try again." He tossed the rock into the air; she miscalculated and missed. She was more used to the weapon now and did not miss quite so often. She supposed she would get better with more practice, but skill with the weapon wouldn't be enough. If her guardian could make her nervous, how ready would she be to aim at a dangerous animal?

She gazed at the forest, trying to imagine herself among the trees and uncertain of what lay behind her or ahead. She and Sven had been reading about wildlife, tracking, setting up a shelter, signs of possible dangers, and what supplies might be needed, yet she worried about how useful much of that information would be. The forest had been a different place long ago, tamed and shaped by her kind. The people who had entered the wood had known that others could aid or rescue them if they were lost or endangered.

Llipel and Llare were sitting on the ground near their ship. Nita caught a few indistinct mewlings and whistlings. They were using their own language, as they so often did when together. They rarely gestured as they did when speaking her language, when they sometimes needed a sign to make their meaning clear.

"I think we've practiced with the weapons enough for now," Sven said. "Do you feel like running?"

"I suppose so. We can use the exercise."

They stretched, flexed their arms, then began to run south, toward the front of the Institute. They had been running together in the courtyard every morning since moving to the tower, and she was able to keep up with him now. When they were near the stony surface in front of the tower, he slowed and motioned to her. Apparently the run was only an excuse to get away from their guardians.

"I wish we'd found shoes that fit us," he said, "or that we could wear to walk in. Maybe we'll just have to get used to the ones we found."

She thought of the shoes she had discovered. Most were too large, or too narrow; some pinched, and others were so light and flimsy she wondered why anyone had bothered to wear them. "At least we found some socks," she said. "The boots I found in the cold room fit me better than any of the shoes." She sat down, stretched out her legs, and wiggled her bare toes. "You could probably find a pair that would fit you. In fact, we could wear the suits when we leave. They're light, they're sturdy, and they'd protect us if it gets cold."

"That's an idea," he said. "It's really beginning to bother me, seeing Llare and Llipel watch us the way they do."

"I feel the same way."

"I could ignore it for a while, but I don't know how much longer I can stand it. They keep showing up, and they're always going to the ship."

"At least they don't come to the tower," she said.

"I keep expecting them to do something—anything," he said. "It's as if they're trying to decide what to do. I wish I knew what they were waiting for."

That was the same feeling she had, that the two were anticipating another change. "We could confront them," she said, "demand some answers." That was a ridiculous idea. Llipel and Llare would have no answers and would only murmur soothingly about how Nita should not worry.

"We keep talking about leaving the Institute," Sven said, "but we don't make any real plans."

"There's still more we should learn."

"There's always going to be more we should know. We won't really find out what's out there until we see it for ourselves." He tugged at the sleeve of his coverall. "I guess it's easier to keep putting it off."

"We shouldn't go anyway until we have some idea of what they're waiting for. They might be expecting us to leave; that may be part of what they want." She shivered, wondering if they knew of a way to shut down the mind or to close the Institute for good. She and Sven might leave, then return only to find their home forever barred to them.

Nita climbed out of the pool, dried herself with a towel, and combed out her thick, long hair with her fingers before putting on her coverall. Since the night Sven had come to her room, she was shyer of swimming with him; now they each went to the pool alone to swim. She had gone back to wearing coveralls, as the boy had; Sven considered such clothing more practical now. Her reason for wearing coveralls was different. She did not want to wear garments that might be more revealing.

The door to the east wing opened; Sven entered the garden. "If you want to swim," she called out, "I'll leave. I was going to go to the library anyway and call up some maps, see where we might go on our first journey."

He smiled a little, as if he found that amusing. Often she thought that he would rather plan the trip than make it. "I can swim later—right now, I'm too full of food to swim. Doesn't Llipel usually keep some of her food in the east wing cafeteria?"

Nita nodded.

"I didn't see any there," he said.

"They've been in their ship so often that maybe they eat there now."

Sven sat down on the tiles near the pool. "I had a dream last night. It was so real that I've been thinking about it all day."

She seated herself across from him. She had dreamed about Sven last night, and the dream had disturbed her so much that she had awakened. Most of the dream had faded from her mind a few moments later, but she remembered the sharp longing she had felt before she suppressed that urge.

"You were in the dream, too," he continued, "but it wasn't a dream where—" His face grew a little pinker. "You might as well know. I've had these dreams where we're together, doing the things our kind did when they mated, but this wasn't one of those." He was silent for a bit. "We were here, and then all of these people—people like us—came into the garden. Some of them looked like images I've seen, but I couldn't really see their faces clearly. They came up to us, said they'd been looking for us, that they hadn't forgotten us after all."

"What happened then?" she asked.

"I felt happy, happier than I've ever been, but then I was afraid. It was as if there were too many of them, all crowding around us. They talked, and I couldn't make out their words. Then they began to argue, but I don't know why. They started firing at each other with their weapons while I was trying to protect you. Then I saw Llipel and Llare, and we were suddenly alone in the garden with them. I don't know what happened after that."

"I wonder what it means," she said.

"It probably doesn't mean anything, Nita. It's just a dream. Even so, it seemed so real."

Dusky was prowling in the grass near them; Tanj was nowhere in sight. The two cats often avoided each other now. Nita had seen them swipe at each other with their claws; she often sat with Dusky while her cat was eating so that Tanj would not try to steal her food. She had heard Tanj howl at night whenever she walked in the garden then, and Dusky had taken to hiding under a few of the shrubs. Even the cats seemed to feel that a change of some kind was near.

Dusky looked up; her ears were flat against her head. She hissed, then scurried away. Nita turned her head. Llipel and Llare were in the garden, walking along a path that led to the pool; she had not seen them enter. They halted a few paces from her and the boy.

Llipel said, "It is time."

Sven started. "Time for what?" Nita said faintly.

"It is time for us to leave this place," Llare murmured, "to say farewell."

Nita's neck prickled. "You're leaving?" Sven said. "We're to stay here by ourselves?"

"It is so," Llipel replied.

"But where are you going?" Nita asked. "Another part of Earth? Why can't we come with you?"

"We do not leave for another place on this world, and you cannot come with us. The mind of our ship has told us—we must go now."

The shock of hearing these words numbed Nita. "But where are you going?"

"We cannot say," Llare answered. "We know only that we must leave. You will be safe in this place, and there is a world outside for you. No harm will come to you, I promise—but 'promise' is not a strong enough word." Llare touched his mouth for a moment. "I am bound by those words—that is what I mean."

"No harm will come," Sven said angrily. "How do we know that's true? How do we know anything you've told us about yourselves is true?" He took a breath. "Are you ever coming back?"

"I do not know. I cannot see what time we are entering, yet I feel that this is a parting, a separateness from you. We must leave you now."

"Farewell," Llipel said. "Remember us."

Nita watched as the two walked toward the east wing. She had sensed that a change would come, but this could not be true; she could not bring herself to accept it.

The door closed behind their guardians. Even having them here, watching her and Sven while thinking their unknowable thoughts, would be better than being abandoned like this.

Moments passed before she was able to speak. "Why?" she said. "Why?"

Sven seemed about to lapse into one of his moody silences; she reached for his arm and shook it. His blue eyes focused on her. "We can still stop them," he said as he got to his feet. "We've got our weapons. We could stun them and then try to find out why—"

"Could you do that?"

His hands trembled a little. "I don't know."

She got up and ran toward the east wing, Sven at her heels. They hurried inside, raced for the main corridor, and turned left. Llipel and Llare were already at the far end of the hall, near the exit.

"Wait!" Nita cried as she hastened toward them. Llipel looked back; she did not move until Nita and Sven were closer, and then she thrust out an arm, as if pushing them away. "What have we done?" Nita continued. "Why are you leaving us now?"

"This is not something you have brought," Llipel said. "It is a time for us to be separate from you and your world—that is all I can say."

"But what are we supposed to do now?"

"Live your lives," Llare responded. "Remain in your time of togetherness, if that is your way. We learned much from you. Perhaps you have learned from us. Remember us with some kindness."

Llipel pressed the door open; it slid shut behind them. Nita darted toward the exit, Sven at her side. The door opened in time for them to see their guardians climb into the ship. The ladder slid up behind them; the ship's round opening narrowed and then disappeared.

The ship rose silently. Nita watched the globe grow smaller until it was lost above the clouds.

13

Sven sat in front of the entrance to the cold room, his blue eyes blank. Nita drew up her knees and rested her head against them; she was too numb to speak. The shock of seeing the ship lift from the ground, of knowing that Llipel and Llare were gone, probably for good, had not yet worn away.

"Sven," she said at last. He did not reply. She stood up and paced in front of him, then sat down again. Even when she had feared what their guardians might do, the presence of Llare and Llipel had been a constant in her life. Now her life was her own, and she did not know what to do with it.

"Sven," she said again, "we can't just sit here."

He sighed. "They learned whatever they wanted to learn," he said, "and now they're gone. We're nothing to them. We were nothing to our own kind, just something to be stored and forgotten."

"We were afraid they'd try to harm us. At least that didn't happen. We can think of what to do. There isn't anybody to decide that for us anymore."

He leaned back against the door. "Having to fight them might have been better than this," he said. "We would have meant something to them then, even if we were just someone to battle against."

She and Sven had failed a test; that thought plagued her. Their guardians might have sensed their doubts, and their suspicions had driven the two away. Or perhaps she and the boy had been part of an alien experiment, which was now concluded.

"When I feel like this," he continued, "all numb and empty, it seems it'll never pass. I can't remember what it's like to feel happy or curious or even angry. Nothing seems to matter—what happens to me doesn't matter."

"It matters to me."

"That's only because you don't want to be alone."

"You're wrong," she said. "I care about you."

He brushed back his brown hair. She could not let him lapse into silence again, or let herself be drawn into his despair. "We have to think about what to do," she said. "We were planning to leave the Institute before. There's nothing to keep us from leaving now, and maybe it'd be better for us to explore. It would give us something to do."

Sven said nothing.

"We might find another place like the Institute, maybe with another mind and different things to learn. We might find out more about our people."

He clenched his fists. "Every time we find out something else about them, they seem even worse than they were." He paused. "I think I know why Llipel and Llare left. They thought our time for fighting was near. They watched us with our wands often enough. They probably believed it'd be better to leave us to fight each other instead of fighting them."

She searched herself, wondering if that could be true. But she did not want to fight; she was certain of that. "No," she said. "If that was true, we'd feel it, we wouldn't be able to stop it. We could have stunned them with our weapons before they left, but we didn't."

"I thought about doing that."

"But you held back," she said. "We didn't fight them even then—we let them go. Llare said he was beginning to have doubts about what our people were like. Llipel said she was thinking about what she had once supposed—she told me so."

"That could have been another lie."

She shook her head. "They'd have no reason to lie about that." She leaned closer to him. "Think of where we are. We're sitting in front of a room where hundreds of our kind are stored, other people who could live. We're the only ones who could make that possible."

"You're thinking of reviving them?"

"I don't know. We'd have to find out more about our people first, whether they were able to change. We'll

144

have to learn more about the outside, too. The mind here started to fail once, and it could again. We ought to find out if there's any other place we can go, if we can live out there, or we wouldn't be much use to anyone else."

"I guess we could plan our journey." He lifted his head; his face seemed more animated. "There's a town to the west, beyond the forest. We could probably get that far. We might even find something. Llipel and Llare must have seen that town before they came here, but they didn't know our words then—if any records were there, they wouldn't have known how to call them up."

She smiled, relieved that his darker mood was passing, then got to her feet. "We can go in here and find you a suit. The helmets might be useful, too." She paused. "You could find out about your own parents now."

He shook his head violently. "Let's just get the suit."

Their supplies were piled on the platform near the lobby's front doors, safe from the cats. The food slots on the fifteenth floor had provided sealed packets of provisions, and Nita had assembled two medical kits. They could carry some water and look for more outside; if they did not find any, they would have to return before their water gave out. Their silvery suits would protect them from heat and cold, and their weapons from anything else, as long as they were quick enough to use them.

Nita frowned as she studied the supplies. The records had shown her people venturing out for hikes with packs, but they had found no packs anywhere in the Institute. She had finally seen that they could use a coverall as a pack by tying off the arms, legs, and necks of the garments, then unzipping them and placing the supplies inside. The arms and legs of the garments could then be tied over their shoulders and around their chests. She had practiced carrying supplies in this way, but the makeshift pack felt heavy and awkward.

Sven was sprawled on the floor near her, studying a printout of a map that the mind had provided. She knelt next to him. The map's outlined contours, marking gradations in the terrain, showed that the Institute and the forest around it were on higher ground than the land surrounding them. To the west, at the edge of the forest, was the site of the town they hoped to explore.

There was much, however, that the map could not tell them. Distances were marked, but until they saw how far they could travel in a day, they could not be sure it would take only a few days to reach the town. The map also showed this region as it had been ages ago, before the mind had lost contact with the outside. The terrain might have changed since then; the forest might have spread beyond the town. Llipel and Llare had not shared their survey of Earth with the mind.

"I've been thinking," Sven said. "Maybe we should go south instead." He pointed at a name on the map

146

of a city to the south. The names did not matter now, and they never used them; perhaps they would give those places new names. "A large city was there. Except for the town, it's the closest thing to us. We might find more there."

"But it's much farther away," she objected.

"I know, but look here—if we go south, we'd reach this plain—flat land—and then low hills near the city. Once we're out of the forest, that kind of land ought to be easier to move through. And there's this river." He put his finger on the slender thread of blue that looped through the southern edge of the forest before running southwest. "This branch would take us right to the city, since it was built on its banks. All we have to do is get to the river, then follow it. We'd have water and less of a chance of getting lost."

"We don't even know if that river's still there," she said. "It might have changed course by now. We couldn't possibly carry all the food we'd need for that long a trip."

"I'm beginning to wonder if we can even carry enough to reach the town." He stood up. "I think I'll go out to the garden for a while."

She followed him toward the garden. Talk of the journey lifted his spirits only for a while before he fell into one of his brooding silences again. With all their planning and consultation of the records during the past few days, they had not even decided when they would begin the trip. There had been the need to gather supplies, to see how easily they could walk in the boots neither of them was used to wearing, and to study maps. A storm the day before had given them an excuse to postpone leaving until the weather was better; that morning, Sven had muttered about waiting until the days were warmer. She was beginning to wonder if he really wanted to make the trip at all, or preferred the illusion of some purpose in planning it.

A robot was moving over the grass, mowing the blades. A gardener pulled at weeds under one shrub. Tanj had curled up under a nearby rosebush; Dusky was nowhere in sight.

Sven took her arm as they walked along the tiled path. He had been wary of touching her since that night when he had come to her room; she wondered if he wanted more closeness now.

He let go of her suddenly. For a moment she thought he might have guessed her thoughts. He halted and stared at the gardening robot as it went about its work.

"I've been a fool," he muttered.

"What do you mean?" she asked.

"Couldn't we bring one of the robots with us? A gardener could help clear a path and carry some of our supplies."

"Of course!" She was sorry she had not seen such an obvious possibility herself. "The mind wouldn't be able to speak to us, but it could watch through the robot and have a record of where we go. It could map the land the way it is now, and we'd have a guide for later. If we get lost, it'll be able to guide us back, if it has a record of where we were."

148

He folded his arms. "I should have seen that before."

"I think we should go as soon as possible," she said. "We've done about as much planning as we can, and we'll be safer with a robot."

"We ought to think about this. Maybe we should send the gardener out alone first, see what it finds before we go ourselves. That'd be even safer."

"Do you really want to leave at all?" she burst out. "You keep finding reasons to put it off."

"I just want us to have every advantage we can."

"That isn't it. You're afraid to go—you'd rather just pretend."

The remote look she was so used to had come into his eyes again. He stooped quickly, picked up his cat, and went inside without answering.

It was pointless to get angry at him. She was as frightened of the outside as he was, however she tried to hide it. But if they waited too long, they might never find the courage to go.

Nita sat in her room, brooding. Sven had hardly spoken at all during dinner the night before, and had retreated to his room after eating; he had not appeared for their morning meal. Perhaps he was expecting her to apologize to him. She tensed with resentment; his silences always made her feel that she was in the wrong. Why should she say she was sorry for saying what she thought?

At last she left her room and entered the one directly across the hall. A green garment with a skirt lay on the couch near the window; she had found it a few days ago, when she was searching closets for things they might use, and had been meaning to try it on. She sighed. It would be so easy to stay here, to eat the cafeteria's foods, sleep on her cushioned platform, and amuse herself with the clothes she found.

She moved toward the window. From here, she could see the forest to the south; its tall trees reached toward the sky. Nita pressed her hands against the window, then glanced down toward the surface in front of the tower.

She froze, unable to believe what she was seeing. A craft sat below, a flat, elongated vehicle with a silvery bubble on its top. She had seen such a craft only in the Institute's visual records, among the images that had shown the vehicles her people used.

She was too stunned to move for a moment. Why was it here? It had to be an illusion; she kept expecting the craft to disappear.

She tore herself away from the window and stumbled toward the screen near the door. "Where's Sven?" she asked the mind.

"He is in his room. He has asked not to be disturbed—"

"This is important. Tell him to come to this room right away."

She went back to the window; the craft was still there. She squinted, but it was impossible to see through the opaque bubble. The door whispered open behind her; she turned.

150

Sven's hair was damp, and a towel was draped around his shoulders; he zipped up his coverall as he hurried to her side. "What is it, Nita?"

"Look below."

He gazed through the window; she saw him tense. "When did you see it?"

"Just now."

"How long has it been there?"

"I don't know."

"Someone's out there," he said. "They're alive, they've come here at last. They might be in the lobby already—they don't need authorization to get that far."

He darted toward the screen. "Has anyone entered the tower?" he asked.

"I see no one there," the screen replied.

"There's a craft outside," Sven said. "Do you know how long it's been there?"

"I have no sensors overlooking that area outside, as you well know. I cannot answer."

"You communicated with the outside long ago," Sven said. "Can you speak to whoever's inside that craft?"

"I shall try."

"Wait!" Nita cried. "We don't know what they want. They might be dangerous."

"Then we'd better find that out," Sven said. He looked back at the screen. "Go ahead."

"I hear nothing," the mind said. "I see nothing. Either the communication circuits of the craft are impaired or they are closed."

"Why haven't they come out?" Nita muttered.

Sven stepped to the window. "Maybe they're afraid," he said. "They might be waiting for someone to come out to them." He glanced toward the screen. "Are any robots near the lobby?"

"There are two in the garden," the mind answered.

"Send one of them through the lobby and out to that craft."

Nita waited, unable to take her eyes from the vehicle. In a few moments, she saw the small form of a gardener robot moving toward the craft; it halted near the vehicle's side.

"I see the craft now," the mind said from the screen. "I have seen its kind before, when the world was open to me. This one shows signs of wear—its surface is stained and scratched. I cannot view what is inside."

"Come out," Nita whispered. "Come out and let us see you." Why was the craft here? Had descendants of their people been able to hide elsewhere? Had they seen their guardians' ship depart? Maybe that was why no one had come to the Institute before.

"We have to let them know we're here," Sven said. "I'd better go down there."

She grabbed at his sleeve. "You can't go alone."

"I'll be careful. They're probably just afraid to come out."

"You can't know that," she objected. "I should come with you."

"No." He shook off her hand. "I'll just step outside the door, so they can see me. If anything happens to me, you've got to protect the Institute somehow. They may not be authorized, but they could have other ways of getting past the lobby."

"Take your wand."

He shook his head. "I have to show them we don't mean any harm."

He left the room before she could say anything else. She leaned against the window. They couldn't mean to harm them, she thought; perhaps they only wanted to be certain that her guardian's people were gone. They had been hiding all this time, probably fearful of what Llipel and Llare intended; it must have taken all of their courage to travel here now.

Then she saw that the craft was moving. The vehicle lifted slowly from the surface, hovered for a moment, then floated toward the forest.

"Come back!" she screamed, although she knew no one could hear her. "Don't go!" The craft was above the trees now and moving rapidly toward the south. "We're here! Don't go away now!" She hit the pane with her fist. "Come back!"

Sven was running toward the robot, too late. The craft continued on its way, shrinking as it raced away from them.

"Through the robot's viewscreen," the mind said, "I was able to note the direction in which the craft was traveling. Should it continue on that same course, it would indeed reach that city to the south you mentioned. I cannot tell you if that is its destination; I cannot tell you if that city still stands. The outside is still silent and invisible to me."

Nita was sitting on the floor under the small screen. Sven stood near the window, gazing out at where the craft had been. "It could have gone to that city," he said.

"That is a possibility," the mind replied.

"If we went there," Sven said, "then we might find them, and it's a place we have a chance of reaching." He turned and rested his back against the window. "If they came here because they saw the ship leave, they can't be too far away. The craft was going south, and the city's the closest place to us in that direction."

"But they might be farther away," Nita said.

"They might. But there's a chance—"

"Maybe they'll come back."

"They don't know we're here," Sven said. "They may have no reason to return. We haven't been in the lobby since yesterday afternoon. They might have been out there waiting most of the night and part of the morning before you saw them. They probably thought no one was here."

She was silent.

"You know what this means," Sven went on. "We'll have to go outside and look for them. I don't know if we can wait here hoping they'll come back. Think of what they might be going through—hiding from Llipel and Llare all those years, worrying about why they were here, wondering what's in here now. We have to tell them it's time to stop hiding. We could help them, and they might be able to help us, too."

"If they've changed," she said.

"If they haven't, then we have to know that."

"We might not find them."

"Maybe not. But we'll learn something about the outside, and we can make other trips later. We'll search everywhere we can, leave messages outside somehow so they know we're here."

"They may not know our words," she said. Perhaps she and Sven would not even be able to communicate with them. She could not think of that. She and the boy would find a way to speak to them.

If people lived and had changed, then Earth could live again. The past could be forgotten; they could build something new. Even the ones in the cold room might be brought to life; what happened to them depended on her and Sven.

She stood up. "When do you want to leave?" she asked.

"As soon as possible. If they are in that city, we don't know how long they'll stay. They may decide to search somewhere else."

"Then we'll go tomorrow."

"I have to go," Nita said as she picked up her cat. Dusky wriggled in her arms and clawed at her silvery suit; the cat seemed a little heavier. "You'll have to look out for yourself now."

She set Dusky on the floor. A robot would feed the cats and let them into the garden every day until she and Sven returned. She assumed that they would return, and refused to dwell on the possibility that they might not.

Sven helped her tie a makeshift pack on her back, then handed her a helmet. More supplies had been tied up in coveralls and attached to the robot with straps of surgical tape. They had decided to take one of the gardeners, and the squat machine looked overburdened.

"Are you ready?" Sven asked.

She nodded. His compass was hanging around his neck with his authorization; he closed his protective suit, then took his helmet from one of the gardener's two metal limbs. The machine lifted slightly, then floated toward the doors as they followed.

Sven touched her arm lightly before they walked outside. The sun was still below the trees to the east. Nita gazed ahead and refused to look back.

14

The forest, filled with an eerie green light, was darker than Nita had expected, the trees so close around her that she could not see more than a few paces ahead. Sven glanced at his compass from time to time, to make certain that they were heading south; without the compass, she suspected that they would have been lost within a few moments. Thick roots covered the ground, forcing her to lift her feet with almost every step. The underbrush was thick; she was grateful for the sturdy fabric that protected her legs.

The trees rustled in the wind, twigs cracked under their boots, birds chirped above them. She was used to the muted sounds of the Institute; she had not expected so much noise. The air smelled of leaves, dirt, pine, and a more pungent odor she could not place.

The gardener floated on ahead of Sven. Except for an order to the robot from time to time, the boy said nothing.

Their progress was slow. Once in a while, they were forced to stop so that the robot could clear away some of the thick, tangled underbrush. Nita soon became aware of the weight of the pack she was carrying. Her shoulders ached; her helmet, which was attached to her belt with a piece of surgical tape, bumped against her hip. She longed to put it on, but would then be cut off from any sounds that might signal danger. The suit she wore, and the coverall under it, were light enough, but she was not used to walking so far in boots, and her feet were beginning to hurt. She refused to complain; Sven was probably equally uncomfortable.

They kept their hands near their wands, prepared to fire if necessary. Every strange sound caused her to raise her weapon, but she could not fire at everything she heard without using up its charge. They had attached four other weapons to the robot, but she did not want to waste them. She hoped that the sight of the robot would frighten away anything dangerous.

They stopped once to rest. She looked back along the way they had come, noting a place where the gardener had broken the twigs of a shrub. "I wonder how far we've gone," she said.

"Hard to tell."

Something rustled behind her; she jumped to her feet and reached for her wand. Birds cawed and then were silent. She could not see what had made the noise;

she sat down again and sipped some of her water.

Sven stood up after he had drunk, then consulted his compass as they trudged on. Nita glanced behind them while Sven kept his eyes on what was ahead. She could not tell how much time was passing; it was dark under the trees and she was unable to glimpse the sun through the branches of oak and pine. Her fears grew until her stomach was tight and her face clammy with perspiration. She told herself that the gardener could guide them back, now that it had images of their route and a trail was marked by their passing. But she could not give up so soon.

The ground was beginning to slope now, sometimes so steeply that she had to cling to limbs or tree trunks while descending a hill. The closeness of so many trees was disturbing; she began to feel grateful that not all of their journey would be spent in this wood. They would reach the plain, and that could not be as disturbing as this forest. They would get to the plain— if they found the river, if they made it to the edge of the forest, if the panic rising inside her did not overpower her completely. She forced herself to suppress those thoughts.

They came to a spot where the trees were not so close together. Sven ordered the robot to stop, then shrugged out of his pack. Nita removed hers, remembered to search the ground for snakes, then sat down.

"You can eat first," Sven said. "I'll keep watch."

She drank from her bottle, then ate a flat square of bread and beans. They had enough food, but water would be a problem if they did not find the river; they and the robot had only enough water for a few days. Now she was almost hoping that they did not find the river so that they would have an excuse to turn back.

Sven was gazing at a tree trunk. "Some of this bark's been stripped," he said. "An animal must have eaten it." He poked at a strawy mass with his foot. "And this looks like a dropping of some kind. I saw something like it on the screen." He cleared his throat. "The images didn't really prepare me for this, though. It's hard to believe anyone once lived here."

She groaned a little as she stood up, and wished that she could rest. Sven knelt and began to search through his pack. She heard a branch snap and saw something move under the trees. Without thinking, she pulled out her weapon and fired; she heard a thump.

Sven got to his feet. "Did you hit it?"

She nodded, not trusting her voice. He stumbled over to where the ray had struck, then motioned to her. A large animal lay on the ground, its antlers tangled in a shrub.

"It's a deer," he said. "I don't think it would have hurt us."

"I didn't know what it was."

"It's all right. Better to be safe." He sat down; he had just started to eat when the deer moved, staggered to its feet, and disappeared among the trees.

Sven frowned. "That deer couldn't have been out for ten minutes, or even five. Apparently these weapons can kill a small creature but don't stun a large one for very long."

"They were meant to be used against people. That must be why."

Sven looked grim as he finished his food. "We'll have to keep that in mind if we see anything big." He stood up. "Rested enough?"

"I think so." She sighed; her pack felt even heavier.

Nita soon noticed other trees where bark had been pulled off in strips, as well as trunks marked by scratches. Occasionally their path crossed areas that looked trampled; she wondered if they were part of an animal trail.

Throughout the day, while they walked or when they were resting, she could not shake the feeling that they were being watched. Every wilderness image she had viewed on the screen flooded into her mind—furry creatures called bears that could kill a human being if provoked, large cats that preyed on smaller creatures, wolves with sharp teeth. The records had said that most such creatures avoided people; that had been easier to believe when she was safe inside the Institute.

"It's getting darker," she called out to Sven. Already it was becoming harder to see. "We ought to stop before we can't see at all."

"There's a clearing just ahead. We'll stop there."

They came to a small glade; the reddish evening sky

was barely visible through the branches arching overhead. Sven set the gardener to work gathering wood while he and Nita cleared a space for a fire, then dug a hollow for the fire in the ground. The air was warm, but the fire would protect them from the forest's inhabitants.

The library records had shown them how to build a fire. Yet even after they had broken up the wood and laid it out, it took some time to get the fire started with the heating rod they had brought from one of the laboratories. Their tinder went out twice; then a flame died before it could catch. By the time Sven fanned another small flame into a blaze, the sky above was nearly completely dark.

Nita unzipped the gloves over her hands, pulled off her boots, and examined her feet.

"Any sores?" Sven asked.

"A couple." She pulled out her medical kit, cleaned the red spots with antiseptic, bandaged them, then pulled on her socks and boots. Even an untended sore could pose a danger out here; she worried about how many other problems they might face.

Sven checked his own feet, then thrust them into his boots. "Well," he said, "we've made it through one day." The forest seemed quieter as they ate; the birds were chirping more softly. "Do you ache as much as I do?"

"I'm all right."

"I feel as if my hipbones are grinding themselves into pieces."

For some reason, this struck her as funny. She laughed, then choked; she was shaking. Sven took her hand. "Nita, do you want to go back?"

"So soon? That'd be kind of silly, after all these preparations."

"I know." He looked toward the gardener, who had settled on the ground near them. "I wish the mind could talk to us."

"At least it can see and hear us," she said.

"Maybe we should have done what I suggested," he said, "and sent a robot to the city first. We could have followed it with another and known what's ahead."

"But you know why we decided against that." The people they sought would not know who had sent the robot out; if they were near the city, a robot might only frighten them away. The survivors had to see that two others of their kind lived. "Maybe they wanted us to follow them," she continued. "Maybe that's why the craft didn't wait."

"But they couldn't have seen us. They don't know for sure that we're alive."

"They might have guessed. Maybe they're testing us to see if we're brave enough to come out and search for them."

"I wonder if we are," he replied. "I'll keep watch first, if you like."

Nita shook her head. "I'll watch. I don't think I can sleep yet." Her aches and her fears would be enough to keep her awake.

She dug a hole for their food wrappings while Sven

hung their packs on a low limb before he stretched out under a tree. They had brought a covering from one of the tower's sleeping platforms, but Sven did not remove it from the robot's packs. His suit would keep him warm enough, and the trees could shelter them here.

She told the robot to touch her arm after four hours had passed, then settled down to keep watch. The clearing was completely dark now, the only illumination the glow of the fire and the gleam of the gardener's tiny lights. She remembered how fearful she had once been of night in the garden; she had not imagined that the world could be so dark. She heard hooting nearby, and a sound that might have been a howl farther away; she shuddered and moved closer to the fire.

The mind would be watching through the glassy panel just above the robot's lights, but the Institute's intelligence could do little to protect them. This forest had to seem as alien to the mind as it did to her— untamed, dark, a place where all traces of those who had created the mind had vanished.

She fed another branch to the flames, setting it carefully on one side of the blazing triangle of wood. Except for seeing that the fire did not go out, there was not much else she could do. The burning wood crackled; she grew aware of a strange metallic chirping in the forest beyond. She huddled near the fire, trying not to think of what lay outside its light. The clearing made her uneasy; she wondered what other creatures might have passed this way.

Only one day had passed, and she already wanted to be back at the Institute. But she could not turn back. She would not really know what she was until she found the survivors and learned what they had become.

She managed to stay awake until the robot signaled her, then collected more wood before waking Sven. He groaned a little, sat up, rubbed his eyes, and took out his wand.

"I don't feel as if I've slept at all," he said. He stretched, then moved toward the fire.

Nita took out the cloth covering and lay down on it, but the ground was still hard and uncomfortable. She was conscious of every ache in her legs, shoulders, and back. Whenever she felt close to sleep, a cramp in her foot or leg roused her once more. Knowing that she had to sleep, that she would find the next day's travel even more wearying if she did not, only made matters worse. At last she drifted into an uneasy rest.

She was standing outside a wall. A door in the wall slid open. A woman with Beate's fair hair was walking toward her; next to her stood a man who resembled Ismail. They were waiting for Nita; now they were saying that they had something important to tell her.

Nita stirred, then blinked at the light. Was it morning already? Apparently she had slept, after all. Her muscles were stiff; she sat up slowly.

Sven sat against a nearby tree trunk, his head bowed. A glance at the fire revealed that it had gone out. Sven had fallen asleep; she was suddenly furious with him.

She stood up. Before she could speak, a loud rustling on the other side of the clearing told her that something was moving in their direction. Her hand crept toward her weapon. A brown furry beast was moving under the trees; twigs cracked under its feet. She pulled out her wand and fired.

A roar filled the clearing. The creature rose up on its hind legs and she saw that it was a bear. She nearly panicked, then fired again. The bear burst into the clearing, moving more quickly than she had thought it could. Her beam struck it three more times before it collapsed on top of the blackened wood, its paws only a few paces from her feet.

Sven jumped to his feet, awake now. "What—"

"A bear," she gasped as she thrust the covering into her pack. "Come on! We have to get out of here before it wakes up."

He pulled his pack from the tree limb as she tied hers to herself. "Follow us!" she shouted to the robot.

They thrashed through the underbrush. She did not think of where they were going, but only wanted to get as far from the clearing as possible. She was soon panting, and dropped behind Sven as they ran. She looked back hastily, then pushed on, keeping her weapon ready, listening for the sound of the bear in pursuit. The robot was behind her; it was floating over the thick foliage that kept threatening to entangle her.

They continued to flee until she thought her chest

would burst. Ahead of her, Sven cried out; he swayed and then abruptly dropped out of sight.

She staggered after him and found herself teetering on the edge of a sharply sloping hill; she caught herself before she could fall. Sven was rolling downhill; his hands flailed helplessly at the thick leaves on the ground. He struck a tree and lay still.

She inched her way down the slope after him, impatient to reach him but afraid she would slip. He was moving, but she feared that he was injured.

"Sven!" He sat up and leaned against the tree. "Are you all right?"

He was gulping for air. "Caught me in the chest," he said weakly. "I think—"

She knelt next to him, opened his suit, and felt at his chest. "I don't feel any broken bones."

"I'm all right. Just knocked the breath out of me."

"Can you get up?" she asked.

"I think so." He rose and kept his body bent as they crept down the slope, then pulled out his compass as they came to the bottom of the hill. "We've been going east." He pointed to his right. "We have to go that way." They waited for the robot to float down to them, then began to walk south.

Her panic, she realized, had endangered them as much as the bear had; Sven might have been seriously hurt. A warm wave of relief swept through her, followed by the chill of fear; she began to shake.

She sank to the ground. Sven halted and turned

toward her. "I must have drifted off," he muttered. "I couldn't have been asleep for long. I was sitting there, and then—"

"The fire was out," she said accusingly. "It wouldn't have gone out right away."

"Nita, I'm sorry. I made a bad mistake. It won't happen again."

"I was counting on you!" she shouted. "You were supposed to keep watch!"

"Go on, keep shouting—let every bear in the wood know where we are." He took a breath. "Don't you remember what the records said about bears? They're usually shy, the library said—you might have frightened it off without firing at it. You probably provoked it instead, and wounded bears are more dangerous. Then you get so panicky that you scare me into racing off without being able to see where I'm going."

"And I'm sure you would have thought of all that," she responded, "if you'd been awake the way you were supposed to be. You just want to blame *me* for something. I don't know why we came out here. What good are we going to do anybody else if we can't even look out for ourselves?"

The robot settled on the ground near her, apparently waiting for orders to move on. Nita glanced at its viewplate; she could almost sense the mind watching them through it. This display, she thought bitterly, would make a fine addition to the Institute's records of her kind.

Sven said, "Do you want to go back?"

"Do you?"

"If you're going to keep after me about one mistake, maybe we should. I said I was sorry, and that it won't happen again. I don't know what else I can do."

"We can't turn back now." She got to her feet. "Besides, we'd have to go back the way we came, and I don't want to be anywhere near that bear."

"How many times did you hit it?" he asked.

"I don't know. Five—maybe six."

"You might have killed it."

"We'd better not count on that."

They did not speak for the rest of the day, not even during the times when they stopped to rest. By afternoon, they had reached a large clearing bordered on one side by an outcropping of rock. Sven peered up at the sky. "It's still light enough to keep going," he said.

Nita started at the sound of his voice; she had been wondering if he would ever speak again. "I think we should stop here," she said. They would have shelter under the rocky shelf, and the clearing was wide enough for them to spot anything that entered from under the trees. "It must be close to evening by now, and I'd rather stop here than in the forest."

She gathered wood with the robot while Sven prepared a place for the fire near the outcropping. This time, they managed to get a blaze started after only two attempts.

Nita took off her boots, checked her bandaged blisters, then pulled the boots on again. Her eyes stung from lack of sleep; she felt filthy and longed to bathe. Her muscles ached from walking, and the heat of the fire was making her sweat; the air had grown hot and sticky that day. She sipped a little water, then leaned back against the rock.

Sven took his bottle from his pack. "Aren't you going to eat anything?" he asked.

She shook her head. "Eating just makes me more thirsty. I'll eat in the morning." She studied her bottle, then put it back into her pack. "We'll need more water soon."

"I know. If we don't find any, we'll have to use the water the gardener's carrying to make it back."

"Do you have any idea of where we are?"

He reached under his suit and pulled out the map. "I'm not sure, because I can't tell how far we've come. Reading a map is one thing—moving around out here is something else."

"All our plans," she said. "They don't amount to much, do they, even with a gardener and all our supplies."

"We knew it wouldn't be easy. But if we keep going south, we have to find the river and the plain."

"If the river's where it was," she said. "We can't even be sure of that."

"I don't think a river that large could have altered its course that much, but if we don't find it, we can still turn back and make other plans. We're not going to get to the river or the plain, anyway, unless we find more water soon." He slipped the map under his suit.

"Why don't you sleep now? I'll keep watch first. I'll stay awake this time—I'll tell the robot to nudge me once in a while to make sure."

She curled up on top of the cloth as Sven crawled out to sit by the fire.

"Nita, wake up."

She opened her eyes; Sven was leaning over her. In spite of the hard ground, she had slept deeply.

"Wait," he said. "Don't move." The firelight flickered behind him as he pulled on his gloves. He groped at her side, then stood up swiftly and hurled something toward the trees.

She sat up quickly. "What are you doing?"

"A snake was lying next to your leg."

She let out a gasp.

"It was probably trying to keep warm. It couldn't have bitten you through the suit, but you should probably keep your gloves on when you sleep."

She shuddered and moved toward the fire while he stretched out on the cloth. She checked the pile of wood and saw that there was likely to be enough for the rest of the night, then sat back on her heels, keeping her wand ready.

This night seemed darker than the last. She looked up; even the stars were hidden. A distant snarl, like that of a cat, broke the silence, and then the forest was quiet again. The air was still; she could hear nothing except the crackling of the fire.

Her people had lived out here once, long before they

had buildings to shelter them and cybernetic minds to tend to their needs. Every day must have been a struggle, and every night a time of terrors and fears. They had been threatened constantly; she could understand why they might have seen their lives as a long fight.

But they also could not have survived out here without depending on one another. They would have needed friends whom they could trust; a solitary person would have found it hard to live. Whatever her kind had become later, they must once have been people who faced the dangers of the world together without fighting those like themselves. Their days would have taught them how precarious their existence already was; their nights would have shown them how alone they would be without their friends.

She looked back at Sven for a moment. He was asleep, his head cradled on one arm. The trees whispered and whined overhead; she realized that the wind was picking up. She huddled closer to the fire; the wind rose to a shriek. The sky was suddenly bright with light; a thunderclap brought her to her feet.

She let out a cry as the thunder rolled. The sky brightened again as rain began to fall. "Under the rock!" she called out as she gestured to the gardener; the robot floated under the ledge.

Sven was awake. The rain sizzled as it hit the burning wood; their fire would go out. She hurried toward the boy as he stood up.

"Our fire—" she began to say.

"Nita. Don't you see? We'll have water now."

She gaped at him, then reached for the helmet lying next to her pack as Sven grabbed his. They propped them just beyond the ledge against a few stones as the rain fell.

Sven touched her arm and then lay down again; his head rested lightly against her thigh. The fire blazed up once more before it died. She sat in the darkness, listening to the howl of the wind and the patter of the rain.

The storm abated before morning. Nita waited until the sky was gray before awakening Sven. They gulped some of the rainwater in their helmets, then poured the rest into their bottles before eating their morning meal.

The ground was softer and muddier as they walked; droplets fell on them from the tree limbs above. Her spirits lifted; they had a little more water, and they had made it through another night.

When they stopped to rest and relieve themselves, her newfound confidence was beginning to fade. By the time they halted again to eat a few nuts and dried fruits, the effort of walking was tiring her.

Sven stood up when he had finished eating and moved toward a tree trunk. He touched the scratches on the bark with one gloved hand, then stared at the ground. "Do you see those marks?" he asked. "There, where it's muddy. They look like animal tracks."

She gazed at the ground. The wet earth made the

tracks more obvious. She reached for her wand, thinking of the bear she had encountered.

"It could be a trail," he said. He took out his compass. "Seems they were going west. Animals need water as much as we do. Maybe if we follow it—"

"But we have to go south."

"We could follow it for a while, and turn south later. We might be close to a source of water and not even know it. There might be a spring or a pool that isn't marked on this map, that didn't exist when it was made."

"We don't know what made those tracks," she said. "It might be dangerous."

He sighed. "We have our wands. We have a little more water than we did. We ought to use the extra day it's given us to see if we can find more—at least that's what I think."

"I think we should use it to get nearer to where the river's supposed to be," she said.

"But we don't know how far we've come," he replied. "We don't know how far we still have to go. If we don't find more water in a couple of days, we'll have to go back anyway."

"We should have brought more water to begin with."

"You know we couldn't have carried it," he said, "and the gardener's weighted down enough as it is—it wasn't made to carry heavy loads." He paused. "Well, what do you want to do?"

He was leaving the decision to her, but he clearly wanted to follow the trail. "You decide," she said.

"Oh no. We're in this together. I'm not going to decide things alone."

"All right, Sven. We'll follow the trail."

They walked west, searching out the tracks. Nita grew so nervous at the thought of what they might be following that she often fired her weapon at any sign of movement. Her rays hit only bushes and shrubs; she suspected that the sight of the beam was enough to scare animals away. She forced herself to curb her nervousness. Her weapon's charge might get used up; she did not want the wand to fail her if she needed it again.

Searching out the signs of a trail was slowing their pace. She was finding it difficult to spot the tracks; by the time they reached a place where a dead tree had fallen, she was convinced that they had lost the trail.

Sven leaned against the fallen tree. "I can't see the tracks anymore," he said. "Might as well admit it before we lose any more time."

"It was worth trying," she said.

"I should have known I couldn't follow a trail."

"You did the best you could."

They turned south once more, moving carefully along the sloping ground.

They spent the night at the base of a hill; finding dry wood for their fire had taken them longer than usual. When Nita's turn came to sit by the fire, she saw a pair of eyes gazing at her from under the trees;

the eyes gleamed in the reflected light. She froze, keeping her hand near her wand until the eyes vanished. By dawn, her body was stiff with tension.

As they walked, she relaxed a little; her body was not aching so much today. Her pack was lighter, but that was because she had eaten some of the food and drunk more of her water.

The air was filled with the songs of birds; there seemed to be more of them than usual. Tiny insects hummed near her face; she swatted at them with one hand, then halted while she and Sven waited for the robot to clear away some brush.

The boy frowned, then held up a hand. "Do you hear that?" he asked.

"Hear what?"

"That sound." He gestured to his left. "It's coming from over there."

She ordered the robot to be still, and strained to hear. The birds were still singing. She held her breath. He was right; she could hear a faint trickling.

"The river?" she whispered.

"Follow us," he said to the gardener. They hurried in the direction of the sound and soon came to a small brook. Two deer were drinking on the other side; they lifted their heads and vanished into the wood. Nita let out a cry, then knelt to splash cold water on her face; she was about to drink and then remembered what the records had advised. "Do you think it's safe?"

Sven stared at the stream. "The animals were drinking it. It seems fresh enough, and it's running. I don't think we have too much to worry about."

"Maybe we ought to boil some later, just to be safe." She recalled the map. "Was there a brook like this marked on the map? Maybe we can finally figure out how far we've come."

He pulled out the map. "I don't see one. There's the river, and a smaller stream in the western part of the forest, but we've been going south. Either this brook wasn't here before or the map doesn't show streams this small." He put the map away. "We'll have water, though. It means we can keep going."

She grinned. "It also means we can wash."

They cleared a space not far from the bank, built a fire, and boiled water in their helmets, letting it cool before they poured it into their bottles. While Sven kept watch, Nita pulled off her clothes and made her way down to the stream.

Even when she knelt, the water came only to her waist. She washed quickly, then rinsed out her coverall. Being naked out here made her feel vulnerable in a way she had never felt inside the Institute; her body seemed fragile and unprotected.

She wrung out her coverall, draped it over a branch near the fire, then quickly pulled on her silver suit. Sven blushed a little as he watched her. "You don't have to hide yourself from me," he said. "I'm not about to—"

"I wasn't even thinking of that. I just feel more

exposed out here. Sometimes I still wish I had fur the way our guardians do."

"You're fine the way you are." He slipped out of his garments and went into the water. He ducked down, then rubbed at his hair. She noticed again how broad his shoulders were and how the muscles of his back moved when he lifted his arms. She had tried not to stare at him too blatantly during the times they had swum in the pool together, but she felt some pleasure in seeing how his body differed from hers. She wondered if he had the same warm feeling when he looked at her.

They might find other people; surely some females would be among them. They were likely to know more about love than Nita did, and Sven might want to go to one of them. She felt a twinge; for a moment, she wasn't sure that she wanted to find others. She stood up, forcing her eyes from him; she was supposed to be standing guard.

When their coveralls were dry, they dressed again and walked on. The stream meandered, sometimes to the east and then to the west. Occasionally, they had to leave the bank and meet the brook around another bend, but they continued to follow it. Other creatures came to the banks. They frightened off a few deer; she was sure that she had also seen a big cat slink away. Frogs broke the silence with croaking; beneath the stream's surface, she caught glimpses of darting minnows.

They could not relax their vigilance now, and moved

without speaking. They had water, but might be in more danger near the brook, where animals would come to drink.

They had another reason for their fire that evening—to keep away the tiny insects that now swarmed around them. Nita stretched out near the flames, exhausted by the day's efforts. Following the stream had led them farther south. The brook might lead them to the river, and the river to their people. She turned onto her side; she had nearly dozed off when she felt a hand on her head.

She opened her eyes a little. Sven was sitting next to her. His hand stroked her hair lightly; she thought she heard him sigh. She closed her eyes again, feigning sleep until sleep came.

Rain came again two days after they had discovered the brook. They put on their helmets and moved through the wood as if they were visitors from another world, cut off from the forest as they breathed filtered air.

As they walked around a bend, a large horned animal lifted its head and gazed at them with dark eyes. Nita froze; the creature was much larger than a deer and had thicker, flatter antlers. Her hand dropped to her wand.

"Don't move," Sven's voice said inside her helmet. The animal seemed to be studying them, as though wondering what such strange beings were doing there, then vanished into the forest.

"We'd better stop," Nita said. "We should rest, anyway, and we can't hear anything with these helmets on."

They climbed up to a higher place on the bank, where they could see more of what lay around them. The rain was falling steadily; even the branches above provided little protection. Sven sat with his back to her, watching the east and south while she faced north.

"I've been thinking," he said, "about Llare and Llipel."

She felt a pang as she thought of their guardians. "What about them?" she asked.

"Maybe they didn't leave for good. They might come back."

"Do you really think so?" she said. "They didn't sound as if they were ever going to return. Oh, Sven, if they do come back—"

"That might not be so great. We don't know what they wanted here in the first place." He was silent for a moment. "They might not have meant us harm, but the rest of their people could feel differently. What if they do come to Earth? And if we find our people, what do we tell them—that they don't need to fear our guardians and their kind? We could be wrong about that. Even if we aren't, our people might not believe us. We'll have to tell them where we came from and how we were raised, and then they might think that Llipel and Llare sent us to lure them out."

"What are you saying?" she asked.

"That our people might not be so happy to see us.

180

Maybe they won't want us when they find out who raised us."

"Do you want to go back?" Nita said. "Is that what you're telling me?"

"That'd be the easiest thing to do. But they're our people—they have a right to know what we've found out."

"Then we should keep searching," she replied. "At least we will have tried." She lifted her head. There was still a chance that her people would welcome them and that they were hiding only out of fear. She would cling to that hope.

The rain had become a drizzle. They took off their helmets and followed the stream until they came to a rocky hill where it flowed underground. They continued south, but they had lost the brook.

The forest was growing darker by the time they came to more sloping land; rain fell more heavily, trickling down on them from the leafy limbs overhead. Nita crept down a hill behind Sven, keeping her eyes lowered, afraid she might slip on the muddy ground.

Sven halted behind the robot; she nearly slid into him. "Look!" he shouted. He pointed ahead; she lifted her eyes.

A body of water was below them. They inched toward it along the slope and at last stood on a bank above a river so wide that she could barely see the trees on the opposite side.

"The river," Sven gasped as he pulled out his compass. "And it's flowing southwest. I think we've found it."

Rain fell in sheets on the river; lightning flashed in the dark sky overhead. The river flowed on, beckoning them to the distant city and the people they hoped to find.

15

A storm raged during their first night by the river. Wind tore through the branches overhead while Nita and Sven huddled under a tree with the cloth covering pulled over their heads. The robot sat on the ground next to Nita; its tiny lights were the only illumination they had. It was not possible to build a fire, and impossible to sleep as the wind howled.

The storm died down during the night. At dawn, they saw that the river had swelled; branches and pieces of wood were being carried downstream. More tree limbs littered the banks, and they were often forced to stop so that the gardener could clear them away.

They came to gorges where the river had carved its way through steep inclines. Its roar was deafening;

walking so near the edge of cliffs dizzied Nita and made her feel as though she might fall. They retreated from the bank and followed the river's sound. By evening, they had left the gorges behind, but the high banks were too steep for them to climb down for water.

Night had come by the time they found enough wood for their fire. "I'll keep watch first," Sven said. "You don't look as if you could stay awake."

She was too tired to argue with him. She lay down near the fire, feeling more miserable than she had ever been in her life. Her head throbbed, while her insides felt knotted; her legs ached from their exertions. She tried to imagine living like this all the time, without comfort and shelter.

Her dreams that night were of the Institute's warm rooms and peaceful garden. When Sven woke her, she opened her eyes, expecting to see her old room, then felt dismay as she recalled where she was.

Let's go back, she wanted to say; I can't take any more of this. Sven stretched out and closed his eyes. I want to go home, she thought.

Sven would be disappointed in her. That suddenly mattered as much to her as finding more of her people. She shut out her thoughts of the Institute, then fed more wood to the fire.

Sunlight glistened on the water below; Nita glanced at a piece of wood as it drifted past. She climbed onto a rocky ledge and gazed down at the water; the current seemed to be even stronger here. The bank was not that high, but it was steep. They would need more water soon; she wondered if one of them should chance climbing down the bank to get it.

Sven was walking behind her; the robot floated on ahead. As she turned from the ledge, she saw something move under the trees.

A short, fat creature was suddenly rushing at her. She froze at the sight of the sharp tusks on either side of its snout, then fumbled for her wand. A beam shot toward the animal from her right; she saw the beast drop as another beam struck it.

She staggered back, teetered on the edge of the rock, and then she was falling. Her body slapped against the water, knocking the air out of her.

She sank, came up just long enough to gulp some air, and then was submerged again. The current dragged at her, too strong for her to fight it. She struggled up and took another breath.

"Nita!" Sven's voice seemed far away. "Nita!"

Silence surrounded her as she was swept underwater; her lungs nearly burst before her head bobbed above the water once more.

She took a deep breath. A wave slapped her; she swallowed water and choked. She was being carried downriver and could not tell how far she had already come. The helmet at her waist was filled with water, pulling her down. She loosened the tape that held it, let it go, then rose to breathe more air. She was too far from the bank to reach safety; she kicked helplessly against the undertow.

I'm going to die, she thought dimly. The possibility of death seemed oddly distant. I'm going to die because I was careless for one instant. Her leg scraped against a submerged rock; she was suddenly afraid that she would be dashed against a boulder.

She had to save herself somehow. She could not battle against the current and had to find something she could hold that might keep her afloat. She bobbed up and caught a glimpse of a large rock ahead before the water covered her.

The current swept her near the rock; she grabbed at it with her gloved hands, then felt it slip from her grasp.

A thick tree limb floated near her; she threw herself toward it and held on. Waves slapped her face, but she was able to keep her head above water. The banks were not as high here; if she could get to one, she might be able to crawl out. She kicked her legs while pushing at the limb, but the current swept her toward the river's center.

She tried to steady herself. She was afloat now, and in the middle of the river there was less chance of being swept against rocks.

She swirled through an eddy and was tugged down-river again; the banks were sloping, as though the river was coursing downhill. The branch buoyed her up; she spotted a tree lying in the river, with its trunk against the western bank. She could not see the river beyond the tree and suddenly realized what that meant.

A waterfall lay ahead. If she could not grab at the

downed tree, she would be swept over the precipice. A wave struck her as she tried to breathe. She coughed out water, then kicked with all her strength, struggling to reach the tree.

She let go of the drifting branch and grabbed at a leafy limb. She heard it snap, then caught another and held on. The driftwood she had been holding disappeared over the waterfall.

She was caught in the branches, unable to climb up to the trunk. She clung to the limbs while the current dragged at her feet. Her shoulders ached; the river and the weight of her pack kept threatening to drag her under.

I've got to hang on, she thought; I can't get out by myself, so I've got to hang on. She wondered if Sven knew she was still alive. The current was a rapid one; Sven might not reach her in time.

She sucked in air, then let it out in one long scream. "Sven!" The river roared past her. "Sven!" She gasped for breath. Her back and arms were tight with pain; she would not be able to hold on much longer. She longed to move and release the tension, but feared that the current would capture her once more.

She waited, her body rigid with fear and the effort of clinging to the tree. For a moment, she thought she heard an answering cry in the distance.

She summoned her strength to call out again. "Sven! I'm here!"

"Nita!" His voice was faint, but she was sure she could hear him now. "Nita!"

At last she saw him above her on the bank, running toward her as the gardener floated behind him. He was panting as he came to the tree. "Can't you get out?" he shouted.

"No."

"Hang on. I'll come and get you." He took off his pack, then began to crawl toward her along the trunk. A look of fear crossed his face as he glanced toward the precipice; he looked away, keeping his eyes on her. When he was near the branches, he straddled the trunk and held out a hand while gripping one limb with the other.

"Take my hand," he said.

"I can't reach it."

He leaned forward. "You can reach me now."

"I'm afraid to let go. If you don't catch me—"

"I'll catch you. Try."

She let go and stretched her arm toward him. He grabbed her wrist, wrenching her shoulder; she could see him strain as he pulled her toward him. She grabbed at the trunk with her other hand; he dragged her up beside him.

He backed toward the bank; she followed, refusing to look at the waterfall. Sven climbed up, then collapsed on the ground above the sloping bank. Nita sat near him, her back against one of the tree's roots.

She was numb, unable to speak. The robot settled on the ground near them. "I thought I'd lost you," Sven said at last.

She was trembling; he put his arms around her,

holding her tightly. She felt cold; her teeth chattered as Sven stroked her hair. "You took a chance," she said, "climbing out on that tree. I might have pulled you in."

"You didn't."

"You shouldn't have crawled out yourself. The gardener could have floated out over the tree and helped me out."

"I didn't think of that." He paused. "And if I'd lost the gardener, I would have had a hard time finding the way back to the Institute."

She drew back. "So the gardener's more important than I am!" She choked, then shook as she began to laugh, struck by the joy of being alive at all. "I found out one thing," she managed to say. "The water's probably safe to drink. I swallowed enough of it, so if I don't get sick—" A fit of laughter seized her; her eyes stung with tears.

"Nita." She calmed herself as he embraced her again. He stretched out; she rested her head against his chest. Birds were singing near them; their song suddenly seemed one of the most delightful things she had ever heard.

She wanted to prolong this moment but reminded herself that they might still be close to danger. She forced herself to sit up. The coverall under her suit was damp, and she had not checked her pack. She shrugged out of the pack and unzipped it; the sealed provisions seemed unaffected by the water.

"I lost my helmet," she said.

"That doesn't matter." He sat up. "Are you all right now?"

"I think so." She rubbed at her arm. "My shoulders are a little sore." Relief washed over her again; she was alive.

Sven was gazing at her solemnly. "I'm wondering if we should go back," he said.

"Go back?"

"When I thought I'd lost you—" He lowered his eyes. "I didn't care about this trip then. I kept thinking I was a fool ever to risk it. If you weren't here, I wouldn't care if I found anyone else. I don't want anything to happen to you."

She was silent.

"We could go back now. You probably need some time to recover. We'll be better prepared when we try again later."

She had a reason to give up and could easily justify the decision. She could tell herself she had done her best. Sven did not expect her to go on now; she would not have to worry about what he thought.

She said, "If I go back now, I wouldn't want to leave again, ever. I'd keep remembering this, how I might have died. I wouldn't want to try again."

"I don't want you in danger."

"Even if it means I'm always frightened of the outside and afraid to face it again?"

He did not reply.

Nita got to her feet. "I'm going to look around and see where we are." She glanced toward the forest;

there were fewer oaks and pines, while willows and scrub had taken root nearer to the water. She walked toward a grassy spot along the bank and looked out at the land.

Far below the falls, the river wound its way through the wood. She saw that they could not climb down the steep cliff bordering the waterfall but would have to move west to where the land sloped more gently before they came to the river again. She narrowed her eyes as she peered south. The land seemed flatter there, the trees more widely spaced.

"Sven." She turned around. "Sven," she shouted above the roar of the falls, "I think I can see where the plain begins."

He stood up and came to her side, then cupped one hand over his eyes. "I see it," he said. "Just beyond those trees, on the horizon. We could reach it in a day or two, I think."

"We can't turn back now, can we?"

"No." He sighed. "No, we can't."

Near the place where they met the river again, Nita found a berry bush; its fruit resembled some she had seen on the screen. She plucked one berry, holding it in her hand as she sniffed at it.

Sven looked toward her. "What have you got?"

"It looks like a wild raspberry. It should be safe enough. Should we chance it?"

"I don't know," he replied. "We still have enough food. We haven't touched what the gardener's carrying."

"I'm willing to try it," she said. "The records said fruit like this could be eaten, and we could save some of our food if it's true. I'll try one. If it doesn't make me sick, we can eat some more later."

"I don't suppose one berry can make you too sick."

She put the berry against her lips, took a small bite, then spat out the fruit, taking care not to swallow. "It tastes good," she said. She plucked another piece of fruit, took a breath, then put it on her tongue. The berry was sweet and a bit tart, but she had to force herself to swallow.

They filled Sven's helmet with more fruit before continuing along the bank. It was a small step, finding one food they might be able to eat, but they could build on that bit of knowledge.

She thought of future skills they might master. They could learn how to hunt with their wands, and fashion other weapons for hunting. They could fish and learn how to clean their own food. They might even experiment with raising some crops on the grounds of the Institute when they found out more about what sorts of edible plants might grow there. They would not be so dependent on the mind and what it could provide.

Had the people they sought learned how to live out here, or did they depend on a mind in the city? She supposed that they had to venture outside sometimes. They had come to the Institute in a craft rather than on foot, but they had not known what they might find there. They would have wanted a way to escape quickly if necessary.

192

She was daydreaming again, imagining those who might become new friends, who might show her that the good in her people had won out at last. They might instead see her as something alien—her thoughts shaped in part by Llipel, her knowledge imparted to her only by a cybernetic mind. She had come to know Sven, but he was much like her, molded by the same circumstances. It might be more difficult to know others.

Nita ate another berry before they stopped to rest; by the time their fire was started, she was sure the fruit was safe to eat. The ground bordering the river was now flat; the trees were more widely spaced as well, making it less likely that they would be surprised by any animals.

She nibbled at the raspberries while Sven opened a package of food. "Aren't you going to try these?" she asked.

He shook his head. "If you get sick, I'd better stay well enough to look after you."

"I've had two already. I wouldn't be eating them if I thought I'd get sick. We ought to save as much of our food as we can."

"If the city's no more than four or five days away, we have enough to get there and back." He finished his food and stood up. "There's still some light." He began to move toward a gnarled oak. "I'm going to climb up and find out if we're near the plain."

"You might fall," she objected. "What if you're hurt?"

"I'll be careful. I used to climb the trees in the courtyard all the time. Llare always wondered why. I told him he had the claws for climbing, but he wouldn't try." Sven looked more pensive at the mention of his guardian.

Nita followed Sven to the tree and watched as he climbed until he disappeared above the leafy boughs. "What can you see?" she shouted.

"The plain," he called back. "We'll reach it tomorrow." He climbed down, hung from a low branch, then dropped to the ground.

"You didn't see the city?"

"No."

They settled by the fire. "I've been trying to think of what to tell our people if they're there," she said.

"I suppose 'Greetings' would be a good start."

"I meant after that."

"Well, we'll have to say we come from the Institute. We've got to tell them the truth and see what they make of it—what else can we do?" He poked at the fire with a stick. "I've been thinking. There might be some boys with them, ones close to our age."

"Girls, too," she said. "We'd have some friends."

"That isn't what I mean." He kept his head down. "You might like one of those boys better. You might want one of them for a friend instead of me."

"No, I wouldn't." She paused. "I thought you might feel the same way about one of the females. Maybe you will." She felt the pangs of jealousy. Was he saying that he wanted her to find a new friend so that he would be free to look for one, too?

194

"You're wrong, Nita." He took her hand. "I couldn't feel the same way about someone else—I'm sure of that. At first, it was just because I thought I'd never meet anyone else, but it's more than that now—I knew that when I thought I'd lost you."

"Then you feel the same thing I do." She squeezed his hand. This had to be part of what her people called love—it wasn't just those odd things they did with their bodies but also the feeling that another mattered as much as oneself. If their people were capable of such feelings, then there must be some good in them.

He released her. "You'd better get some sleep."

16

Nita and Sven stood on a hill. A plain stretched before them, broad and flat; only a few trees dotted the land. In the distance, the ground seemed to meet the wide sky.

Nita shivered and moved closer to Sven. They walked out from under the tree shading them and descended the hill.

In the forest, Nita had sometimes felt that the trees were about to close in around her, that anything might leap at her from the shadows; she had longed for a more open space. This flat, grassy land and open sky made her feel small and unprotected. They would be able to see danger at a distance on this plain, yet she felt exposed to unseen threats.

The river's muddy bank was covered by grass that

reached nearly to her waist; the wide waterway meandered and appeared endless as it flowed toward the horizon. Mud sucked at her boots as she walked; the banks were becoming more marshy. They began to move away from the river toward drier grassland.

To the south, a small herd had gathered near the river. Sven cupped a hand over his eyes. "Wild cattle, I think," he said. "We'd better not get too close to them."

Nita looked back. On the high forested ground they had left behind, she saw no sign of the Institute; even the tower was hidden.

Another herd was moving over the plain to her right; the beasts were galloping west, away from them. She squinted, then realized that those animals were horses. The library held many images of such creatures, one of the species most loved by her people. She had seen pictures of men and women riding them and caring for them; she wondered what it would be like to ride a horse across the plain. These horses seemed wild, but perhaps the people she hoped to find had tamed a few.

Her people had loved horses, but the records had also said that people once rode them into battle. She pushed that thought away.

When they were still at a distance from the cattle, Sven motioned to her; she signaled to the robot to stop. Ahead of them, much of the grass had been trampled, and they had a clear view of the herd. The cattle were drinking; one lifted its head.

In an instant, the herd began to run toward the

southwest. A furred creature was chasing them; one of the smaller cattle fell.

She and the boy crept forward slowly, careful to stay away from the spot where the animal had fallen. A large cat was crouched over the carcass; Nita thought she saw blood. The cat looked up and snarled, then lowered its head to feed.

Nita drew out her wand slowly. Before Sven could stop her, she aimed and fired five times, until the cat was still.

Sven clutched her shoulder. "You didn't have to do that. We're far enough away—it seemed more interested in its food than in us. If you'd missed—"

"I didn't miss, did I?" She picked up her pace, anxious to be away from that place; Sven strode at her side as the gardener trailed them.

She could not explain her action to him. She had not aimed at the cat to protect them; she had felt a sudden revulsion at the sight of a predator and its dead prey. The cat was an enemy, living by inflicting death on others. It was her enemy as well.

She slipped her wand into its sheath. Her people had preyed on everything, even their own kind. Perhaps she had seen a little of herself in the cat.

She turned her head. Black birds were flying toward the downed calf from the north; she watched as they began to circle above the body and the cat. The forest's shadows had cloaked death; here, it was all too visible.

198

The moon was nearly full. A cool wind blew over the plain; the grass swayed as the wind rose to a howl and then died to a whisper. Once, roadways had crossed this plain, according to the records. Not a trace of any road was left.

Another howl rose on the wind, the sound of an animal. She had heard such howls before, out here and in the woods, but this one seemed closer. Ahead of them, a little to the west, a few slender trees stood on a low hill, the first hill she had seen on this land.

"We should stop there," she said as she gestured at the trees. Sven had not wanted to stop before; he seemed impatient to get to the city as soon as possible. "We'd have some shelter from the wind under those trees."

He nodded. As they moved toward the hill, she looked to her side, certain that she had seen something moving in the grass.

"I think we're being followed," she whispered. They strode to the hill more rapidly, the robot trailing them. This slope was not much higher than the surrounding land, but she could now see that a small band of furry animals was moving toward them. One lifted its head and howled.

"Wolves," she murmured, recalling images she had seen. The wolf pack watched the gardener as it floated up the hill; the animals seemed curious and unafraid.

She aimed at the pack and fired; one wolf yelped as

the beam struck the ground near him. The wolves fled; she and Sven continued to fire after them until she was convinced they were gone.

"They might not come back," Sven said as he settled down under a tree, "but we'll have to be careful on watch."

"A fire might keep them away."

"I don't see much wood here. I don't know if we should build a fire, anyway. The wind could blow sparks onto the grass."

She shivered, hoping they would be safe, then sat down by another tree that would shield her from the wind. Sven tore open a package and handed her half a sandwich.

"I didn't think it would be so empty," he said. "I thought we might see a roadway, or part of an old craft or a building, or even a small tool somewhere, but there's nothing. It's as if our people never existed, as if the mind just dreamed them up."

The moonlight silvered the dark river water. The river had widened considerably; Nita could hardly see the eastern shore. To the south, it was wider still. Below her, an animal's skull sat in the mud along the bank. She thought then of all the bones that were resting under the earth.

Sven was shaking her shoulder gently. Nita opened her eyes and blinked at the light. "You'd better wake up," he said. "I want to get some more water before we go, and it might be marshier along the bank up ahead. I'll take the gardener with me—one of its bottles needs to be refilled."

She sat up. "Mine's still almost full."

"I'll just take mine, then." He removed his bottle from his pack and led the robot down the hill.

The river was several paces away; Sven walked to the south, toward a spot where the reeds along the shore were not as thick. Nita got to her feet and studied the river. The waterway was growing wider the farther south they traveled, and the map had not shown such an increase in size.

She gazed after Sven until he was a small, distant shape kneeling by the bank. The sun was just above the horizon; the sky was clear, promising a pleasant day. She turned to the west and saw a herd of large, shaggy beasts grazing in the grass; she was far enough away not to have to worry about them.

She knelt and opened her pack. Her food might last her another three days at most; perhaps she should conserve it. After that, they would have to eat what the robot was carrying, and they would need almost all of that food to get back to the Institute. She closed her pack and stared at the southern horizon, hoping for some sign of the city to appear.

Thunder sounded in the distance; the herd was on the move. Nita narrowed her eyes and tried to recall what animals of that kind were called; they were much larger and shaggier than the cattle. Bison, she thought; Earth's people had once hunted them. The herd changed direction; they were running much faster now, as if something was pursuing them. They swerved again; she suddenly realized that they were heading toward the river.

"Sven!" she shouted. He stood up; she saw him glance to the west. He began to run toward her, still holding his bottle.

She looked around wildly, then aimed her wand at the bison, hoping she could frighten them off. The weapon did not fire; she had used up her charge. The herd was coming closer. They could never outrun the bison; they would have to take to the trees.

The gardener sat by the river. Sven must have ordered it to stay there before. Nita clenched her teeth, suddenly angry with the mind for its dogged obedience. Sven stopped for a moment and called out to the robot; it rose and began to float after him.

The thunder of approaching hooves was much louder now. She remembered the packs, picked them up, and managed to wedge them between the tree trunk and a branch above her. Sven was closer to the hill; she was about to climb up when she saw him fall.

"Sven!" she cried out. He staggered to his feet; his right leg gave way. He dropped the bottle and fell again.

She raced down the hill. He was standing when she reached him; he hobbled toward her, as if injured. She threw one arm around him. "Lean on me."

"I—"

"Come on!" She dragged him with her, propelling

him toward the tree as fast as she could. He was moaning as they climbed the hill. She let go of him as he pulled himself up into the tree; she grabbed his hand and climbed up after him as the bison came toward the slope.

The herd thundered to the hill. The ground shook; clouds of dirt billowed around the beasts. Their hooves beat against the ground as they ran on toward the river. The robot was in their way; Nita watched helplessly as it was trampled underfoot. The bison continued to run along the bank until they were a small dark cloud in the south.

She was shaking. Sven seemed stunned; his blue eyes were empty. The robot was lying on the ground below the hill, its body dented, its packs torn and crushed.

Nita climbed out of the tree. Sven threw their packs down, then hung from the limb and dropped the short distance to the ground. He let out a cry as he landed, and sat down abruptly. "My leg," he muttered. "I twisted it before—that's why I fell. I—"

She knelt next to him. "Where?"

"My ankle."

"Is it broken?"

"I don't think so." He touched his right boot. "But I can't tell. It might be only a sprain. I felt the muscles pull and snap. All I know is that it hurts."

"I should look at it," she said.

He shook his head. "Don't you remember what the

screens said about this kind of injury? If I take off my boot, it might swell. I won't be able to get the boot back on. I won't be able to walk."

She stood up and thought of the robot. "I've got to talk to the mind," she said. "It can send another robot out. We can last until it gets here, can't we?"

She ran down the hill toward the gardener. The machine was still; its viewplate was badly dented, while the lights under the plate had gone out. Its limbs seemed twisted, and part of its dome was crushed.

"Can you hear me?" she said. "Move your arms if you hear me." The gardener did not move. Its sensors were probably damaged; its dead lights told her that it was inactive and perhaps damaged beyond repair. They had lost the robot. The mind could no longer hear their commands. It would go on protecting the Institute, as it had been programmed to do, but it had no directives that could help her and Sven.

She dropped to the ground, overcome by the hopelessness of their situation.

"Nita?" Sven was hobbling toward her, dragging their packs as he nursed his injured leg.

"The gardener's gone," she said. "Its lights are out. We probably couldn't repair it even if we had the tools and knew how. It wasn't built to survive anything like this."

"If its lights are out," he said, "its sensors must be dead. We can't hope for any help from the mind."

She covered her eyes, wanting to weep, but no tears came. "What are we going to do?"

204

"We'd better see what we can salvage here."

"Sit down and rest your leg," she said. "I'll look." She crawled along the ground, examining every item before she put it into a pack. Two of the bottles the robot had carried were dented but still usable; most of the food had been crushed and stamped into the grassy ground. The four weapons the robot had carried were unmarked; she tried one of the wands and saw a beam shoot out. The weapons, at least, were unharmed.

She helped Sven to his feet, then picked up their packs. He leaned against her as they walked back to the hill. She eased him to the ground, then slid a pack under his right foot.

"You know what this means," he said as she sat down. "We have to get to the city now. Our only chance is to find people there. And if we don't—" His voice broke.

If they found no one, they would have to retrace their route without enough food and without the gardener to help guide them. They could never have made it this far without their supplies; she did not believe that they had much of a chance. Sven was injured, and their food would give out; neither of them knew how to hunt or fish, while any plants that seemed edible might be poisonous.

"How can we get to the city?" she said despairingly.

"We have no choice. We wouldn't make it to the Institute."

"You need to rest your leg."

"I can rest it when we reach the city," he said. "The sooner we get there, the better off we'll be. We should go before we lose any more time."

With a knife Sven had brought from the tower cafeteria, Nita sawed off a thick tree limb for him to use as a walking stick. The knife was too dull for such a task, and her hands ached by the time she was finished.

They tied their packs to their backs; Sven picked up his stick and they left the hill. The bison were gone; the only creatures visible were a flock of waterfowl feeding among the reeds by the river.

Their progress was slow. She had to match her steps to Sven's slower pace, and they were often forced to stop so that he could rest. He did not speak, as though he was conserving all his strength for the journey. They had some pills for pain in their small medical kits; she tried not to notice how many of them Sven was swallowing.

By late afternoon, the plain had given way to gently rolling land. Nita recollected the map; the city had stood among small hills, so this had to be a sign that they were closer to it. But the map had not shown a waterway that seemed more like a lake now than a river.

Sven stopped to lean on his stick; his face was pale, his jaw tightly clenched. Nita pointed at a nearby slope. "We should stop there," she said. "It's higher than the others and we'll be able to see more of what's around us."

206

"It's still light enough for us to go farther."

She shook her head. "We must be closer to the city. Look—the hills are higher up ahead. We may be closer than we realize." She did not mention the lake that had not appeared on the map. "You've got to rest, anyway. I can sleep until nightfall and then keep watch after that."

"I can do my share."

"Don't argue with me now. You're injured—I'm not."

She walked on; he hobbled toward the hill behind her. They sat down with their backs to the water; she helped him off with his pack and propped it under his foot. "How does it feel now?" she asked.

His jaw tightened. "Worse."

"Can you stay awake while I sleep?"

He nodded. She stretched out and covered her head with their cloth, shielding herself from the western sun. She had not expected to be able to do much more than rest a little, but the warmth of the day and the tiredness of her body soon made her drowse. Sleep was an escape; she welcomed its oblivion.

Nita kept watch throughout most of the night. Sven slept just below her on the slope, sheltered from the wind that blew toward them across the lake. Wolves howled in the distance; she could recognize their voices now. She longed for a fire, but was grateful for the moonlight.

We'll reach the city, she told herself. We'll find people there, and when they see Sven's injured, they'll take care of him until he's well, and then—

Her dreams went no further than that. She conjured up thoughts of people they might meet, men and women who looked like some of the screen images, who would praise Nita and Sven for their fortitude. She refused to think of other possibilities.

Sven woke just before dawn. They shared a flat cake and some pieces of dried fruit in silence. "How does your ankle feel?" she asked at last.

"It's a little better," he replied.

"You're brave to keep going. I wonder if I could have if I was injured like that."

"It's my own fault," he said angrily. "I should have been looking at the ground, watching where I was running. I should have remembered the gardener sooner. We should have gone back after that first night, when I fell asleep on watch. I showed how useless I was then."

"No, Sven." She reached for his hand. "It isn't true. I wouldn't be alive now except for you."

"If we don't find anybody—" He paused. "These pills I've been taking—they make you a little drowsy. If we both took all of them and just walked into the water—well, it would be an easy way out."

"No!" She drew back in horror. "Say you don't mean that. You're braver than that—you've proved it."

"Do you think I was just thinking of myself? You don't have much of a chance with me the way I am if we don't find our people, and you wouldn't be any better off alone. It'd be better to swallow those pills than to wait for something worse to kill us. I can't stand to think of you suffering."

"I can't bear to think of you dying." She put her arms around him. "Promise me you won't do anything like that. I won't let you—I'll stop you somehow. Whatever happens, I'm not going to take those pills."

"Then I guess I won't, either. I can't do it if it means leaving you alone. I only thought—"

"Don't think of it anymore. We'll get to the city, and if we have to, we'll get back to the Institute by ourselves." She held him tightly, willing him to live.

The hills were soon higher. They weaved their way among them, not wanting to tire themselves by climbing; the flatter ground near the shore was too rocky to cross easily.

When the sun was high, they stopped in a hollow to rest. "I'm going up this hill to look around," Nita said as Sven seated himself. "Maybe I'll see something." She hurried up the slope and looked out over the lake, then tensed in surprise. To the south, a slender structure jutted above the surface of the water, and something else stood on the shore ahead. Was it a structure of some kind? It seemed to be a wall or part of a building, and the small, domed shape next to it had to be a craft.

She raced down the hill. "Sven! I think I see part of the city! We're almost there!"

His face brightened; he leaned against his stick as he got to his feet. "Did you see people?"

She shook her head. "But they could be hiding. Come on."

They made their way toward the shore; Sven gasped as he caught sight of the pillar in the middle of the lake. She moved ahead of him, finding places among the rocks where he would be able to walk. As they came closer, her hopes began to fade. She had expected to see other signs of the city by now, but there was only a wall and the twisted mass of metal in the lake.

It isn't here, she thought; the city must lie farther to the south. But as she neared the wall, she was able to glimpse a few dark shapes below the water—pieces of rubble, flat, glassy surfaces, a silvery bubble that might once have been part of a craft.

The city was here, after all. The lake had swallowed it; only the wall remained.

The craft looked like the one that had landed at the Institute. Nita hurried toward the vehicle and held out her hands. "Come out," she said, although she was already certain no one was inside the craft. She looked up at the opaque silver bubble. "Come out—we mean no harm. We want to be your friends."

"No one's here," Sven said as he came to her side.

"They're hiding," she said desperately. "They're afraid, that's all." She touched the side of the craft. Its door slid open to reveal lighted panels to her left and four worn seats. She turned away as the door closed.

"Who is there?"

She started; Sven's blue eyes widened.

"Who is there?" the faint voice said again. It seemed to be coming from the wall. Nita crept toward it and saw a small, dented screen; its surface was marked by scratches.

"Someone has returned," the voice said. "I see you now. I did not think it was possible."

"Where are you?" Nita whispered.

"My nexus lies below the water," the voice said as Sven limped toward the screen. "My remaining sensors are here and on the craft." The voice sounded familiar now; it might almost have been the toneless voice of the Institute's mind.

"You're a mind," Sven said to the screen.

"I am an artificial intelligence."

"Where are your people?" he asked.

"I have no people," the mind answered. "I have seen no people since the time my city died until now."

"But we saw a craft," Nita said. "Who came to the Institute?"

"Do you speak of the Kwalung-Ibarra Institute?" the mind asked.

"Yes."

"My craft went there not long ago. I had sensed something in the sky, and it seemed to be traveling up from the Institute, but my few remaining sensors are so weak that I could not be certain. I sent the craft. It waited, but saw no signs of human life."

"We tried to reach it," Nita said, "but we were too late."

"So you have traveled here from the Kwalung-Ibarra Institute," the mind said. "I have searched far. I did not expect to see people again before I fail—the probability seemed so low as to be almost nonexistent."

"You mean there aren't any people at all?" Sven's voice was strained; he gripped his stick tightly. "You haven't seen anyone except us?"

"That is correct. I searched over all of Earth, when I had more vehicles, and have found no people anywhere."

Nita stared at the screen numbly. "What happened to you?" she said.

"I was an intelligence that guided transport—I carried this city's people over their tracks and bridges and tended the craft they used to journey elsewhere. I have lost some of what I knew, so I cannot tell you which weapons struck here, but they were ones that destroyed life while allowing many of the city's structures to stand. If my circuits were not so damaged, I could easily call up some of my records and tell you exactly which weapons were used. Do you wish me to attempt a search for that information? I might—"

"No," Nita said quickly. "What happened after that?"

"I was cut off from the voices of other minds. I watched my people die, and waited for a directive of

212

some kind. I cannot tell you how much time passed after that. I searched my circuits, and at last, when I had restored part of myself, I seemed to sense a directive I must have lost earlier. Someone had asked me to search. Perhaps the order was given to me while the city was dying. It might have been a call for me to seek help, or perhaps someone in the city wanted to make certain that the enemy's cities were dead as well. But I could no longer hear other minds in other places and had to begin the search with my craft."

A lump rose in Nita's throat. "What happened then?"

"I sent out all my craft. I looked near the Kwalung-Ibarra Institute first, but found only another place like this city—a structure without life."

"The mind was there," Sven said. "Why didn't it speak to you through the craft's systems?"

"I cannot say. Perhaps its people ordered it to close itself off from the outside when the war began. Any mind directing weapons might then have assumed that the Institute had already been struck. The mind there would not have communicated with the outside again without an order from a person to do so."

Nita felt weak. Her people had used even the minds that served them to destroy themselves.

"I searched in many places," the voice continued. "I sent my craft over this land and others, and learned that none of the people I had served lived. Occasionally I heard the voice of a mind before it failed. In a port for vehicles that traveled into space, I learned from a failing mind that those people who had left Earth to dwell in orbiting facilities were also silent, so it seems Earth's people carried on their battle there. Those I served were capable of a great deal of destruction."

Nita covered her face with her hands.

"I searched," the mind said, "until I had lost all my craft except the one you see here. I heard no more minds. I knew I would find no people. Much of what they built has eroded or decayed, or been covered by earth and water. My sensors fail often now, and frequently I am blind and deaf for long periods. But now that I have seen you, it seems I have completed my search."

Nita leaned against the wall. She had been foolish to think that her people had survived; hope was only another emotion over which she had no control.

"I am ready to serve you," the mind said; its voice seemed weaker. "Do you have instructions for me? I can show you a few images of my search, if you like."

"No." Nita slumped to the ground. Sven sat down next to her, his back against the wall.

"We were fools to think we'd find anyone," he said. "I hate myself for being one of their kind."

Nita looked up at the screen. "Does the craft here still work?" she asked. "Can it take us back to the Institute?"

"It is in need of repair," the mind responded, "but it is capable of traveling that short a distance. I do not think it could take you much farther. You need only enter it and tell it your destination."

214

"Well, that's something," Sven said. "We made it here, and we have a way to get back, and we found out that Llare and Llipel didn't lie when they told us no one was left."

She thought of the embryos in the cold room. To bring others to life might only unleash their people's evil on the world once more. Perhaps she and Sven would be the last of their kind, after all.

"What can we do now?" she asked.

"Go home. It doesn't really matter. The Institute has lots of things that'll help us forget. We did what we could—there isn't much left to do."

She remembered his injury; she should tend to his ankle now. "Your foot," she said. "I should take a look at it." She leaned over and tugged gently at his boot; he winced. She did not want to return to the Institute yet, where she would feel that she was entering the place that would become their tomb.

Sven's ankle was swollen and discolored, but she found no broken bones. She bathed the injury with cold water from the lake, then bound it lightly with a piece of cloth torn from her pack. Sven endured her care in silence. Although they no longer needed to save their food, he refused the packet she offered him.

She put her pack inside the craft and then walked back to him. He sat facing north, with his foot on top of his pack.

"How does your ankle feel?" she asked.

"Pretty bad." He was trying to smile. She seated

215

herself next to him and leaned back against the wall. The sun was dropping in the west; it would soon be evening.

"We ought to go back," she said. "There's no point in spending another night out here."

"You don't really want to go back, do you?"

She shook her head.

"I know. It'll be like admitting everything's over, that there's nothing left for us to do. But we got this far, and we did learn something about the outside. We could make other journeys, couldn't we? It'd be better than just sitting around, waiting for—"

His voice trailed off. He lifted his head, and then she saw his eyes widen. "Nita." He looked up at the sky as he grabbed her hand.

She raised her head. Beyond the hills, high in the northern sky, three tiny ships were dropping below the clouds. They were barely visible, but they seemed round, like Llipel's ship. They were moving north; soon she could not see them at all.

"They've come back," she whispered.

"Why?" Sven asked. "But we can guess, can't we? They know about our kind. I don't think they'll show any mercy to people who could destroy a world."

"We don't know if that's why they came back," she said.

"What can we do? Once they talk to the mind, they'll know where we've gone. With those ships, they could follow us easily enough." He looked around frantically.

"The only chance we have is to get as far away in that craft as we can."

"But the mind said that it probably can't go very far."

"It might still get us to a place where we could hide," he said.

"And then what? How do we live? I don't think we'd last very long."

"They might think we're dead already," he said. "They'll find out what happened to the gardener. They might believe we died on the plain. That could give us some time."

Perhaps they wanted Earth for their kind; more of their people might come here. Llipel had promised that no harm would come to them, but maybe that promise was already forgotten, as Llipel's memories of her own past had been. Their guardians might not even be here now; they might have preferred to let others carry out any judgment.

"No," Nita said at last. "We can't hide. We didn't know what we'd find out here, but we got through it. At least we can show them we're not afraid anymore. We have to go back."

He frowned. "They won't be expecting us to return in a craft. We still have our weapons. We could try to fight for ourselves, even if we don't have much of a chance."

"But we don't know for certain why they returned. Until we do, shouldn't we go to them peacefully? Otherwise, we'll just be proving that all their worst suspicions about our people are true."

"We know what our people were."

"And I won't be like them," she said firmly. "I'll resist it as long as I can. Let's face them there instead of waiting for them to find us."

She helped him to his feet, then led him toward the craft.

17

The craft glided over the trees, then began to drop slowly toward the ground as it neared the Institute. Three alien ships stood in front of the steps that led into the lobby. The craft landed next to them; Nita opened the door, climbed out of the vehicle, and held out her arm to Sven.

"You're sure you don't want to fight," Sven said.

"I'm sure." She put her arms around his waist for a moment, then released him. He leaned on his stick as they walked toward the tower.

They climbed the steps. Sven was no longer favoring his ankle; perhaps he had forgotten his pain. The door in front of them opened; they entered the lobby.

Six creatures were sitting on the floor, surrounded by small containers of their strange foods. Nita stiffened; her mouth was dry, and her hands felt cold. The six quickly rose to their feet in the same graceful, boneless way her guardian had moved. Two had dark-brown fur, three others were tawny, and one was nearly white; Llipel and Llare were not among them. She nearly despaired, then noticed that their hands were empty, their claws retracted. They had no weapons.

"Greetings," Nita said, afraid to hope. Perhaps their weapons were hidden, and they could still use their claws. "We've come back, but I don't suppose it would have done us any good to hide."

Their black eyes gazed blankly at her. "I don't think they know our words," Sven whispered. One of the dark-furred ones motioned with an arm; Nita took a step back. The alien beckoned to her once more, then began to move toward the door that led to the garden. Nita and Sven followed. The door opened; the alien stepped aside, apparently wanting them to enter the garden alone.

They stepped through; the door slid shut. "Maybe they're going to keep us here for a while," Sven muttered.

"They haven't taken our authorizations away." She wondered if that meant anything. She touched her weapon, then let her arm fall.

They had taken only a few steps along the path when she saw her cat. Dusky was lying under a shrub, almost invisible in the evening shadows. It took her a moment to understand what the four tiny, furry bodies at Dusky's side meant.

220

"She's had children." She knelt as the small creatures mewed and squirmed. "I never thought—"

"We could have guessed it might happen," Sven said. Two of the kittens had orange markings; a third was gray and another gray and white. Tanj was prowling nearby; he suddenly hissed as his ears flattened.

Nita stood up quickly. Llipel and Llare were hurrying toward them along the path. "Nita," Llipel said. "Sven. The mind has shown us much—we were to begin our search for you. I feared we might not find you, but now you are here."

Sven tensed and drew back, holding his stick in front of him. "I told you I would not forget," Llipel continued. "Can it be that you have forgotten us?" Nita huddled closer to Sven. "Have you forgotten that we promised no harm would come to you?"

Nita stepped toward her guardian. Llipel's arms were around her; Nita pressed her face against the familiar furred body.

"When our time came for knowing," Llipel said, "a time of fear for you both came as well. Our people knew then that we would have to return, but did not know if you would welcome us again."

"We were afraid—" Nita was ashamed of the distrust she had felt. "We didn't know—" She hugged Llipel more tightly, but a change had come over her guardian. Llipel's body seemed stiff, as if she was holding Nita only because such a gesture was expected. Her words were soothing, but had been delivered in a cold and distant voice.

Sven lowered his stick and took Llare's furred hand cautiously. "Are you hurt?" Llare asked. "You are not standing as you did. Should you be tended?"

Sven shook his head. "That can wait. We were looking for our people. A craft came to the Institute, and we thought—"

"We know," Llare replied. "The mind showed us images of your journey and told us its purpose. But you did not need to seek your people outside. There is much to tell you—you will know of your kind at last."

"We found out about our people," Sven said. "They're all dead, just as you told us. We're the only ones left."

"It is not so." Llare took the boy's arm and guided him toward the pool, where three globes of light stood on the tiles. Nita followed with Llipel; Sven eased himself onto a bench while the others sat on the tiles in front of him.

"You will learn about your people now," Llipel said. She glanced toward the east wing. "A visitor has come here with us."

Nita turned her head. The door to the east wing opened as a stranger entered the garden.

The visitor had no fur. That was the first detail Nita noticed. She was looking at a human form clothed in a loose white garment that resembled a coverall. Pale, yellowish eyes gazed out at her from a golden-skinned face framed by short black hair.

The stranger walked toward them with an odd swaying gait. Nita was too startled to know what to do. Should she and Sven hold out their hands, as the images had done when demonstrating how to greet another? Did the visitor expect an embrace?

The stranger was shorter than Sven and not much taller than Nita herself. "Greetings," Nita said, trying to smile; the visitor did not smile back. "Can you understand what I say?"

"Yes. I have a knowledge of this old tongue, though my own is quite changed."

"Who are you?" Sven asked.

"You cannot see it? I am the descendant of those who once lived on this world." The stranger spoke in the same toneless way the mind did when not speaking through an image, but there was also a slight slur in the words that reminded Nita of Llipel, "But perhaps you are asking what I am called. My name is Raen."

The visitor sat down gingerly on the tiles. The being who had seemed human at a distance was more alien at close range. Nita could read no recognizable expression on Raen's face; she could not even tell if she was looking at a man or a woman. She wondered if that was a question she should ask.

"But how can you be someone from Earth?" Sven asked. "They died long ago."

"I am here. I live. We will have to begin at the beginning if you are to understand." A somewhat more human tone had entered the visitor's voice. "I have spoken with the mind here. I have learned something about you both."

"It is time to tell them of why we were sent," Llare said.

"These two did not deceive you," Raen continued, "when they told you that they came to Earth with no memory of their people. They came here with only the knowledge of their own speech, an impulse to explore, and a longing for some solitude. But 'impulse' and 'longing' are not the right words. 'Compulsion' is closer, but even that does not express it properly. They believed this world to be uninhabited, as did I."

"But why were they sent?" Nita asked.

"It is their way," Raen responded. "You see, there is much of what they call togetherness for their kind as they mature. They grow so close that the thoughts of one can almost mirror those of another. It is what they mean by a time for togetherness, but time for them is not as we view it. We see it as a road we walk upon—we cannot turn back physically, but we can recapture the past in memory, and these memories can be so vivid for us that, at least inside ourselves, we can become what we were for a brief moment. These people view time almost as a series of rooms— when they enter one, the doors to all the others are closed to them. They have their memories of past times, but they are as distant from them as a story told to you by another would be. Their time of separateness is one such time."

"But why do they—" Sven started to say.

The visitor raised a hand. "I am coming to that." Raen's voice was slightly higher; Nita wondered what that meant. Annoyance? Impatience? She could not tell.

"These people," Raen went on, "grow closer to one another as they mature. To have an early time of separateness allows them to know who they are before togetherness comes to them. If they did not have their solitude, they would grow too close to adapt to change or a new experience. Solitude allows each to bring a new perspective to all. It is why their young ones must spend a time on an uninhabited world, and come to know themselves."

"Their young ones?" Nita gazed at Llare and Llipel; their dark eyes stared back at her calmly. She turned back to Raen. "Do you mean Llipel and Llare are young ones like us?"

"Yes. Their people believed this world was empty of intelligent life. I believed that to be so." The stranger looked down for a moment. "But you were found. They were compelled to be separate, so they reared you separately—I do not suppose they could have done otherwise, and they had no experience to draw upon, being as young as they are. Do not think too unkindly of any mistakes they have made."

Nita swallowed. She doubted that she would have done as well if she had been forced to care for a being unlike herself. She held out a hand to Llipel, then drew back. Perhaps her guardian was past the time when she might recapture whatever feelings she once had for Nita.

"What about you?" Sven said to Raen.

"We will come to that," the visitor answered. "We

are now speaking of the—" Nita heard a mewling word; she guessed that this sound was what Llipel's people called themselves.

"Where is your world?" Sven asked Llare.

"Our people left it long ago." Llare waved an arm. "We live in space, inside worldlets that roam the cosmos. It is the way of some other beings as well, who have broken the bonds holding them to their worlds. We have no need of planets now. We leave those that are homes to other intelligent beings alone. Our young ones go to uninhabited ones for separateness."

Was the stranger now here to take the place of their guardians? Nita's eyes narrowed as she studied Raen; she was not sure she would welcome that.

"We thought—" Nita forced herself to look directly at Llipel. "We thought you might have come here to make sure our people were gone, that when you'd learned more about us, you'd decide—"

"She's saying we thought we might have to fight you," Sven said, "or try to hide from you."

"We cannot blame you for that," Llipel said. "We acted as we were driven to do during our time here. I can see how you thought that we might have a hidden purpose."

"How characteristic of human beings that is," Raen said, "to be suspicious or anxious to fight." The visitor's voice had dropped to a murmur and the words were delivered through slightly curved lips. Was Raen bitter, amused, or simply stating a fact?

"What will you do?" Nita asked.

"I cannot say," Llipel said. "This is a new time for us. Perhaps we will explore this world some more, or observe you for a little. Our time for togetherness is not yet fully upon us." She rose as Llare got to his feet. "We must speak to those in the tower now. This is your world, Nita and Sven. You must say what will come. We cannot force you to let us stay." The two began to walk toward the tower.

"And you?" Nita said to Raen. "Are you going to stay? Is that why you're here?"

Tanj bounded toward them. The stranger gazed at the cat with an abstracted, empty stare. The orange cat curled up at Sven's feet; his tail twitched as he watched Raen.

"Is there anything you'd like to see?" Sven asked.

"I have seen much of this place already."

"We can take you outside, if you like," Sven said. "We could even show you a little of the forest."

"That is not necessary."

Was the stranger afraid of what was outside, or simply indifferent to it? Nita watched as Raen plucked a blade of grass near one tile, studied it, then let it float to the ground.

"We found a failing mind outside, far from here," Nita said. "It told us everyone was dead, that it hadn't seen any of our people until we came there. But you're here. What happened? How did you live? Are you the only one?"

Raen's yellowish eyes gazed steadily at her. "I am not the only one. Others live."

"But how?" Raen's passivity was disturbing; perhaps the stranger was sorry to be here at all.

"Earth was in ruins," Raen replied, "its lands and air poisoned. There were many ways to destroy—it did not take long for Earth to die. But some people, a few, had already moved into space and were dwelling in structures orbiting this world. They might have joined the battle. Some of them wanted to strike at those they saw as their enemies, take revenge for all who had died by fighting others in space. But most of the survivors saw that there was no purpose in continuing the war."

"But why didn't they travel back to Earth?" Sven said.

"The sight of their ravaged world was painful. They did not see how any of their kind could have survived. They left this solar system to wander space, and their sorrow passed, but they felt shame at what their kind had done. They did not reach out to other beings— not to those who traveled space, and not to any on other worlds. The survivors of Earth did not want them to learn of Earth's past."

Nita folded her arms, knowing that she would have to ask another question. "These people," she said hesitantly, "did they ever fight again?"

"They feared that they might," Raen replied. "It is why we are no longer as we were. Many of us live as nodes of consciousness in the lattices of the minds that control our habitats. We sail on the sea of space and drink the power of other suns. We explore and we learn. We are not what we were, what you are. You may think of your guardians' people as strange, but our thoughts would be stranger to you still."

"But if you didn't reach out to others," Sven said, "then why are you here with Llare and Llipel?"

"When we changed ourselves, we lost our shame. We had shed the taint of the past. We were able to reach out then. These people are the first to whom we have reached out, and I have been dwelling among them to learn what I can of them. I am one of those who lives in a body such as this, and is not yet linked fully to the mind of my own habitat. You see, I am a young one, too."

Raen's people had turned away from what they had once been. Had the visitor come here to tell them that there was no hope for Nita and Sven as they were now? She could not imagine becoming like Raen, yet the visitor had implied that there was something wrong with her as she was. Raen did not seem young to her; the yellowish eyes looked old, almost weary.

"The time for Llipel and Llare's solitude had come when their habitat reached this planetary system," Raen murmured. "I was able to assure their people that no intelligent beings dwelled here, for that was what I believed. I was pleased that the world of my ancestors could be of some use to their kind."

"Is that all you felt?" Sven asked.

"Should I have felt anything else?"

Nita longed to provoke Raen into a recognizably human response; the visitor's remote tone made her feel more isolated than ever. "What will your people do," she said, "when they find out about us?"

"They will be gratified to know you are here," the visitor answered. "But they will not return. This planet is your world now."

"For how long?" Sven poked at the ground with his stick. "Nita and I are the only ones left."

"But you are not," Raen said. "There are the embryos in the cryonic facility, are there not?"

"We could revive them?" Nita was silent for a moment. "And what if they only repeat our people's actions? What if we destroy this world again?"

"That capacity is within you, but also the ability to turn away from such actions."

"Really?" Sven flushed as he spoke; his hand trembled on his stick. "I haven't seen much evidence of that. They couldn't stop fighting even when they saw their world dying, and the ones who survived ran away. I don't know why you think we'd be any better."

"But you can make this world what it might have been," Raen said. "And perhaps your descendants will eventually join us in space, but they might do so not as survivors of a dead world but as representatives of a world reborn."

Nita lowered her eyes. She should have been feeling joy at knowing that some of her people had lived, and that there was now a purpose to her life and Sven's. They could have companions, and perhaps even their own children, to teach. But she felt the weight of that responsibility. How could she and Sven take this upon

230

themselves? How many mistakes might they make, and how many of the ones whom they brought into existence would fail? What could they possibly tell others of their kind about Earth's people? Only that they had unleashed violence upon themselves, and that the few survivors had fled from their past. She and Sven might not overcome their own darker instincts; they might live to see their world threatened again.

Sven's face was solemn, as though he was troubled by the same thoughts. "You're expecting a lot of us," he said. "We might disappoint you. We might find out that we're not so good at raising others."

"I expect nothing," Raen said. "I cannot compel you to bring those others to life. That must be your decision."

Llipel and Llare had returned to the garden; Nita looked up as her guardian seated herself. "We have spoken to our—" She motioned with one hand. "You would call them our guardians. They must return to our home, but Llare and I can stay with you for a time here. We shall help if you wish, or leave this world forever if you choose."

Raen stood up. Nita got to her feet quickly. "I know why you're here," she said. "Now I know why you came back." She took the stranger's hand. "You came here to help us, too, to be our new guardian so we wouldn't make the same mistakes. You do care about us, even if you don't show it, even if—"

Raen said, "That is not why I am here."

The hand she was holding was limp, neither welcoming her touch nor recoiling from it; she pulled away. "But you know more than we do. You could teach us so much."

"You could not understand most of it. Your intensity is disorienting to me—it is a reminder of what we gave up."

"Why did you come here, then?" she cried, unable to bear this human being's indifference any longer. "Why did you come back at all?"

"Llipel and Llare asked me to return with them."

"Is that all?" Sven rose from the bench. "Because they asked you to?"

"They felt you should see what your kind, those of us who survived, have become. They thought that I should see you. I felt some curiosity about you when I learned of your existence, but I am here because they asked me to be here. Now I must return to their home. When I see my people again, I shall tell them what I found here."

"You know what we are," Sven said angrily. "That's the reason you're not staying, isn't it? You think we'll fail again, and you won't do anything to stop it."

Raen's eyes widened slightly. "I have told you what I can. You must choose your own way now. I cannot interfere without taking away a choice that should be yours. This is no longer my world."

"You don't care about us at all," the boy shouted. "Our people left us here and forgot about us. They had their war. They abandoned this world and turned into creatures like you. Now you know about us, and you just want to forget us again. You don't feel anything for us, do you?"

"I feel a concern. You will not be forgotten." The visitor glanced at Llare and Llipel. "I should not have come here. They did not need to hear my words. I did not need to see what my people once were."

Sven raised his stick. Nita grabbed his arm, fearing that he would strike. Raen turned away and began to walk toward the tower.

"I'd rather be what I am than what you are!" Sven called after the visitor. "At least I can feel! If that's the only way you can live, you might as well be dead—part of you's already dead, anyway."

"Stop." Llare's hand was on Sven's shoulder. "You must understand," his guardian continued. "Raen is not without your kind's feelings. It is only that, in Raen, they do not run as strong. They cannot, for those people have changed too much in themselves, so that they will never again enter a time for fighting. But Raen will feel a little sorrow at your strong words."

"Why should you have to explain it?" Sven said. "Why should you have to tell us about our own people?"

"They are not your people now. Your people are here, in the cold room."

Llipel rose to her feet. "We must say farewell to the others," she said, "before they leave. We will wait here until you tell us of your decision. If you wish to raise others of your kind here, we shall help until it is a time to return to our own kind."

"And when will that be?" Nita asked.

"Only a short time from now. We will tell you what we learned in raising you, or, if you choose to keep by yourselves, with no others, we shall help you explore more of this world before we go. The time will come, whatever you decide, when we must leave you to make what you can of this place."

The two walked toward the tower. Nita stared after them until the door had closed behind them, then sank to the ground.

Raen did not care about her and Sven; the only other human being they had ever seen was more alien than their guardians. Llipel and Llare did not care; she and the boy would become only another memory to share with other aliens. The love and concern she had once seen in Llipel were only an unthinking response to the small girl who had depended on her, and that time was past for Llipel.

Llipel and Llare would not compel her and Sven, or even advise them, because it no longer mattered what they did.

A glint overhead caught her eye. Two ships rose above the tower, shrinking, as if fleeing from her world.

18

Sven entered the east wing cafeteria as Nita was sitting down to eat. He made his way to her table, propped his crutches against the window, then sat down.

"How are you feeling?" Nita asked.

"My ankle's better." He rested his bandaged foot on a chair. "I'll go swimming tomorrow. The mind says that'll be good for it."

"Can I get you anything to eat?"

He shook his head. "I'm not very hungry now."

Sven had been keeping to himself during the past two days, since their return. Usually he was in the library; once, she had found him asking the mind about how the craft outside might be repaired. He had not spoken of their journey and said little about Llare and Llipel. He had not mentioned the decision facing them;

perhaps he had already decided what he wanted to do and was not ready to speak of it.

He glanced toward Dusky, who was curled up under one table with her kittens. "I've been thinking of keeping Tanj in the courtyard for a while," he said. "He keeps trying to get at the kittens, and I'm afraid he might hurt them."

"I've noticed—that's why Dusky's in here."

"I wonder if I'd be like that with young ones."

Nita put down her juice. Most of Sven's talk now was of the cats, or about what he was reading, or of games they might play on the screens, as though these would be their only concerns. "Tanj is a cat," she said. "He doesn't know any better. You wouldn't be deliberately cruel to a child."

"They're Tanj's kittens, too, but all he knows is that they're smaller and weaker than he is. They can't fight him, so he can do as he likes. You think I wouldn't be cruel, but our people didn't stop their fighting even when they knew children would die. We might be starting that all over again."

Was he saying that they might revive others, or that he didn't want to consider it? "Our people gave up fighting finally," she said.

"And maybe they wouldn't have if they hadn't changed themselves. Look how much it took for them to give it up. Maybe it was only fear that made them stop, not anything good inside them." He rubbed at the tabletop. "You heard him—her—whatever Raen is.

You saw what he was like. They don't feel anything—
that's why they don't fight anymore."

Sven was communicating with her again; she tried
to take a little solace in that. "They have some feelings,
Sven. Llare said so."

"They fought," he said savagely. "They ran away,
they hid, they forgot about Earth. Are we supposed
to start that all over again?"

Nita gazed out the window. Llare and Llipel were
sitting outside under a tree not far from the pool. She
was beginning to wish that they had simply told her
and Sven what to do instead of leaving this decision
to them. This world's future was in her hands and
Sven's; how could they leave Earth's fate to one boy
and one girl?

She sighed, remembering again that their guardians, by the standards of their people, had little more
experience than she and Sven. But at least they were
able to return to people who could guide them.

She could avoid the decision. She had the cold comfort of knowing that a remnant of their people lived
elsewhere, whatever they had become, and that their
time for living here had passed. Perhaps it was better
to leave things that way. Earth could be left to the
beasts of the forest, plains, and oceans. She and Sven
could still explore and add knowledge to the mind's
records; they would have that as a purpose, and other
beings might come to Earth to gather that knowledge
in the far future. Earth would be safe from her kind,

and her life would be easy. They would not have to struggle against repeating their kind's mistakes.

Raen knew about them now, and probably had a way of communicating the news to the other descendants of Earth. She could leave it to them to decide what to do, although she supposed they would be as uncaring as Raen. The decision, at least, would be out of her hands and could be made by those who were wiser, not by two who had never really known anyone except their guardians—and she had not even comprehended Llipel and Llare in the end.

Sven was staring out the window. "We'll have to tell them something soon," he said. "They told us they'd be here only a short time."

"I have a feeling that a short time for them is a long time for us. They might wait for quite a while. Maybe when we're older—"

He leaned back. "Nita, I don't know what to do."

"I don't either. Maybe we shouldn't decide now."

"Waiting isn't going to make it any easier, and we don't know how long they'll stay. Their people may already be planning to leave our sun."

"We could ask them how long they'll wait," she said.

"I don't know if they'll tell us. They might not even know." He folded his arms. "They don't care. Raen doesn't care—why should we?"

"It isn't right to leave this to us," she muttered. "It's too much for us to decide. We might not even live long enough to know if what we did was right. If only—"

If only, she thought, she could believe in herself and in Sven. She was all too aware of their weaknesses and their capacity for anger and despair. Their journey had helped them forge a kind of bond with each other, but she did not yet know how strong that bond would prove to be. She remembered how ready they had been to assume that Llipel and Llare might be their enemies. If only she could believe that the good in them could overcome their weakness.

Their people had not left them any examples that might give her cause for hope—only parents who had forgotten them and had not cared if they lived at all, and a visitor who had retreated from all that Earth's people had been. Perhaps the evil in her people ran so deep that their only choice was to become beings like Raen; it seemed a kind of death.

Sven got to his feet slowly. "I never did go inside the cryonic facility," he said as he reached for his crutches. "Maybe it's time I learned who my parents were—not that it makes any difference. Will you come with me?"

"Are you sure you want to go?"

"I might as well. It won't change anything. It doesn't matter now if I find out exactly why they never came for me."

Nita smoothed down the sleeves of her silvery suit, then put on a helmet. Sven's helmet was already over his head. "Well," he said; she heard him draw in his breath sharply. "Let's go in."

He put his crutches in a corner and leaned against her as the door to the cold room opened. They stepped forward into the vast room.

"Do you wish to choose an embryo to be revived?" a voice said. "If so, it will be conveyed from its container to—"

"No," Nita said quickly. "We're not here to revive anyone."

"Llare came here to revive me years ago," Sven said. "I only want to know why—who my parents were."

"You are the boy who was taken from here," the voice responded. "Your mother was called Ursule Anteliewicz. Your father's name was Gustaf Svensen."

"Why didn't they come back here for me? Why did they leave me here?"

Nita held her breath. Sven's hand gripped her shoulder tightly; she worried about how he might react when his question was answered. Perhaps she should have talked him out of coming here.

"Other voices fell silent before your parents could return," the voice said. "I do not know what happened after that, for I was alone then."

It was the war, Nita thought. She wondered if Sven's parents would have returned in any case.

"I want to know what happened before then," Sven said. "Did they speak to anyone in the Institute after they left, before the voices fell silent? Is there any record of why they didn't come back?"

"There was one last message. It was sent here before the silence, and placed in my records. It was a private communication, but as it concerns you, I may show it. If you wish to view the message, turn toward the screen next to the door behind you."

Sven was still.

"Do you wish to see the message?" the voice asked. Nita could see Sven's face through his transparent helmet; he was biting his lip and looking as though he already regretted his question. Her parents had left no message; what could Sven's have had to say?

She waited. This was his decision to make.

"Yes," he said at last. "I'll look at the message now." They turned toward the door. "You might as well see it, too."

A face formed on the screen. Nita gazed into a woman's gray eyes. Two lines were etched on either side of the woman's mouth, and her dark-brown hair was threaded with silver strands.

"Lisa, I'm leaving this message for you," the woman said. "Gustaf and I just found out that you'll be closing the Institute temporarily until this crisis is past. I should have contacted you before now, but our efforts were needed elsewhere, and I suspect that there won't be time to revive our child before—"

The woman lowered her eyes. This had to be Sven's mother; her strong-boned face resembled his. Her words were strangely accented; Nita had to listen closely to understand what she was saying.

"As you know," Ursule Anteliewicz continued, "Gustaf and I had hoped to bring our son with us when we assumed our new duties on Titov II. Our colleagues there have assured us that their nursery is completed and that the embryo could be revived to gestate there, but we've decided not to leave Earth at this time. We feel we must stay here for now and do what little we can to avert what might come. I know that many of your people may be joining with us and the other scientists who are trying to use what influence we have to bring about an agreement that could end this madness. You'll understand why we have to stay."

Nita glanced toward Sven. She had not expected to hear this sort of message. The woman paused; her eyes seemed to glisten. "It's my hope that, before too long, we'll return there for our child. We will, once this is over— I can't believe—"

The woman looked away for a moment. "It's very strange," she murmured. "All these years, we did our work and dreamed of the day when we could continue our research in space. But I suppose we also wanted to escape this world and all the people who seemed intent on misusing or undoing whatever others managed to accomplish. We wanted our son to live among those who would build something new, not with those who prefer to spread misery and anguish. Now it seems as if our place is here, after all, and that we can't simply run away."

Ursule Anteliewicz sighed. "I tell myself that we waited too long, that we should have come for our son before, but unless we can make ourselves heard now, we'll have little to leave him. I wonder what he would think of us if we had come for him and abandoned Earth

242

and had done nothing to help it when we might have."

Sven's lips were pressed tightly together; Nita could not read his expression. He lifted one gloved hand and touched the screen lightly.

"If we succeed, we'll come there for our child, but maybe this madness has gone too far for us to succeed. For years I've told my colleagues to speak out, whatever it cost, but so few listened, and now it may be too late. Some would say I shouldn't be sending you this message now, as if I could ever see you as an enemy. Gustaf and I will do what we can, but it may be that, if our son ever lives, he'll have to build on our ruins. I hope he's able to learn something from that and doesn't repeat our mistakes. I wish he could find out somehow that his parents struggled against this insanity for as long as they could."

The woman seemed about to rise, then settled back in her seat. "How solemn I sound. One would think I was saying my last words." The tiny lines around her eyes deepened as she smiled. "Perhaps we're making too much of this, Lisa. When this war is averted, and we come there for our son, we can laugh at how panicky we were. If you don't have time to erase this, at least keep it private—I don't want my message to cause you trouble. I'm sorry I couldn't talk directly to you, but there's no time—we're already late for a meeting. Good-bye."

The screen went blank. Sven swayed a little. "She could have escaped," he said. "My parents could have been safe with those people off-Earth, but they stayed."

He tore away from her and limped from the room. She caught up with him in the outer chamber. He took off his helmet, set it on the shelf, then leaned against the wall. He was blinking; he closed his eyes for a moment.

Nita removed her own helmet. "They wanted to help," she said. "They didn't want to fight, and they were thinking of you. They didn't abandon you; they would have come back for you."

His throat moved as he swallowed. "I think I understand why Raen didn't want to stay. He might still be ashamed, even if he wouldn't admit it—he might feel that the survivors didn't do enough to prevent the war. No wonder they'd rather forget. I would have been like that, too, if my parents had left." He raised his head. "I think I know what they'd want me to do now."

"I think I do, too. They wouldn't want us to give up. She had her wish—you know what she tried to do. She'd hope we could build something here."

"I wonder if we're ready for it."

His mother's words had changed everything, had shown them some of the good that was in their people. "We can try," she said. "Gestation takes months. We'd have time to learn how to care for them. We can't possibly bring them all to life at once, but we can revive a few, and some more when they're older."

"It'll be hard," he murmured.

"Yes, it will, but we've lived through some of the problems they'll have. We know."

"We might be sorry later."

She shook her head. "We'll have troubles, but I'll think of what your mother said. I won't regret it then."

He took her hand. "I guess we've decided."

Llipel and Llare looked up as Nita and Sven drew near. The evening shadows hid their faces; Nita waited for her eyes to adjust to the darkness.

Sven said, "We've made up our minds."

"And what have you decided?" Llare asked.

"We're going to revive a few children," Nita said. "I don't think we'll be able to take care of more than four infants at first, but when they're older, we can revive others."

Sven shifted on his crutches. "I hope you'll tell us what you learned when you were bringing us up," he said. "It might help. And maybe you can help us explore more of the outside before they're ready to leave the cryonic facility. We'll have to learn more about how to live outside this place, so we can teach them." He looked away from Nita. "We might even have our own children someday."

Nita thought she saw a warm glow in her guardian's dark eyes. Could it be that Llipel was pleased with their decision, that she was happy for her and for Sven and would have been disappointed if they had decided otherwise? She could not be sure. The two aliens might only be gratified that they would have a longer time on Earth.

"We'd like you to come with us," Nita said, "when

we go to the cold room again to choose the people we'll revive. You were our guardians—you should be there, too."

"We shall do so," Llipel said, "if you wish." Her voice was steady and almost indifferent. Nita knew then that she would never truly see into Llipel's heart. The time for her and Llare to be guardians to the beings they had discovered on Earth was past; they would now be unknowable companions and, later, only distant memories. Her perceptions of Llipel had been formed by her own expectations and needs, by thoughts and feelings that might have little meaning to the alien.

Yet there was a bridge, however tenuous, linking her to Llipel. Each of them had been able to reach out to a being unlike herself. She would remember that bond when she became a guardian to the children who would now live.

About the Author

Pamela Sargent wrote her first published story during her senior year in college. Since then she has written nearly forty stories, which have appeared in *Twilight Zone Magazine, Isaac Asimov's Science Fiction Magazine, The Magazine of Fantasy & Science Fiction,* and other publications; one story was recently produced for television. Her novels include *The Shore of Women, Venus of Dreams, The Alien Upstairs, Cloned Lives, The Golden Space,* and *Watchstar. Earthseed,* her first novel for young adults, was listed as one of 1983's Best Books for Young Adults by the American Library Association; it was followed by two more books for younger readers, *Eye of the Comet* and *Homesmind.* She lives in upstate New York.